So This Is Love
Miyeko May

Contents

Dedication . . . 1

Author's Note . . . 2

PLAYLIST . . . 3

1. Laila . . . 5

2. Laila . . . 17

3. Sonny . . . 26

4. Laila . . . 33

5. Sonny . . . 45

6. Laila . . . 59

7. Sonny . . . 68

8. Laila . . . 80

9. Laila . . . 93

10. Sonny . . . 106

11. Laila . . . 115

12. Laila . . . 128

13. Sonny   141

14. Laila   147

15. Laila   161

16. Sonny   168

17. Sonny   181

18. Laila   190

19. Laila   195

20. Sonny   202

21. Laila   205

22. Laila   212

23. Laila   225

24. Sonny   231

25. Sonny   239

26. Sonny   250

27. Laila   251

28. Laila   257

29. Sonny   264

30. Sonny   269

31. Laila   275

32. Laila   280

You deserve love.

Author's Note

This story features sensitive topics including parental loss, pregnancy loss, grief and toxic parents. Please take care of yourself while reading.

PLAYLIST

dec 11th – giveon

can i be him – james arthur

this city – sam fischer

sleep at night – cat burns

special – sza

lonely – justin bieber, benny blanco

everything – ella mai, john legend

make you mine – giveon

they don't know – jon b.

forever – rod wave

this is – ella mai

i luv her – glorilla, t pain

1
Laila

I SILENTLY CURSE MYSELF for not grabbing my jacket before stepping outside in the cool October air, but I don't dare to go back inside to find it. I'd rather be out here shivering than accidentally run into Martin, my boss, before my shift starts. I only have a few minutes before I'm supposed to clock in but I savor these moments of calm before what I know will be a long night. With each exhale my breath is visible for a moment before it disappears into the air.

My phone buzzes and I pull it from my pocket to see an incoming FaceTime from my best friend Zara. As soon as the call connects and she fills the screen she is speaking, her words tumbling out quickly.

"Hey, do you know where my black knee high boots are? I've looked everywhere and I can't find them."

From what I can see Zara is standing in the bathroom of our apartment as she gets ready for the concert. Her makeup is flawlessly applied, accentuating all of her features. The false lashes and gold shimmer in her eyeshadow makes her round eyes pop and the brown gloss draws your attention to her full lips.

"I'm not sure," I answer. "Did you check under your bed?"

Zara leaves her phone propped up on the bathroom counter while she goes off screen and back to her room to check for the shoes. When she comes back a moment later she triumphantly holds the boots in her hand before she bends down to put them on.

"Okay how do I look?"

She does a slow turn so I can see her outfit from all angles. She's dressed in a black mini skirt and a small black halter top, minimal jewelry and the boots that she called me looking for.

"You look fine as hell you know that!" I reply, hyping her up.

"Thanks boo," she says, blowing me a kiss and giving me a small wink.

I laugh at her, switching the phone from one hand to the other so that I can use my hand to rub my arm against the cold.

"You got all dressed up just for the concert?"

"The girls and I might go out after too but also who knows he might see me from the stage and instantly fall in love with me," Zara replies.

I shake my head at her and giggle. "Well if he picks you out of all the thousands of other girls, just let me know what color I'm wearing to stand up there next to you at your wedding."

"My chances could be high, its his hometown show" she says as she leaves the bathroom to get her jacket and purse.

I still think her chances are less than none, but I keep the thought to myself. If it were to happen to anyone, it'd be Zara. She has a magnetic energy about her and I've never met anyone who didn't like her.

"You are coming out with me and the girls tonight right?"

"I can't, I have a paper that was due tonight that my professor gave me an extension on but ---"

"Oh shit the ride share is downstairs," Zara interrupts as she frantically moves around the apartment gathering her things to leave, damn near giving me whiplash from her frantic camera movements. "Okay, I love you, I'll see you later tonight!"

Just as quickly as she appeared, she's gone, the call ending. I lean back against the building, feeling the coolness of the brick seeping through the back of my T-shirt. I fold my arms over my chest, rubbing my hands over my bare arms to try to generate a bit of warmth against the brisk wind. I only have a few more minutes before I have to be inside so I try to enjoy the silence, even if I am freezing my ass off in the process.

I only last outside in the cold a little while longer. With a deep sigh I grab the handle to the door and yank it open to go back inside. Inside the building is still cold, no doubt to try to combat the body heat of all the people here to see the concert. I used the back hallways to get to this specific door to go outside in an effort to get away from the growing crowd arriving for the show. I'm sure most people don't even know these hallways exist, seeing as they're usually empty. In the distance I hear voices but I can't make out any of the words that are being said. I reach the end of the first hallway and round the corner to the next one that will lead me back to the general areas of the building when a door on my right flys open. The sound of door slamming against the wall startles me, and I freeze right where I stand. A guy storms out of the thrown open door and another follows close behind, both of their backs to me.

"That contract is fucking bullshit, and you know it Bryan!" the man yells, anger radiating off of his body.

He's dressed in a dark gray hoodie and joggers. The hood is pulled up on his head, so I can't see his face, but even from how far away I am I can tell he's tall, over 6 feet.

I press myself up against the wall at my end of the hallway in an attempt to not make myself more noticeable than I already am. I want to give them privacy for their heated conversation, but since the only way back to where I need to go is past them, I'm stuck here.

"I know, I know and I'm working on it," the other guy, Bryan, says calmly. He's in dress pants and loafers with a button down shirt, the top few buttons left open and the sleeves rolled up.

"Then get it done," the first guy seethes. "Don't come to me with these bullshit offers."

"The team and I are doing everything we can to get you what you want, but you have to work with us and give us more time to do our jobs," Brian tries to explain.

"Bringing me these low ball offers is not doing your damn job. Don't tell me you're trying, either get it done or I'll find someone else who will."

Bryan tries to speak but the other guy holds up a hand to stop him.

"I don't give a fuck what you have to say right now. Just give me a fucking minute aight?"

Bryan gives a curt nod before he goes back through the door that they exited earlier, pulling it closed behind him.

I let out a small chuckle in disbelief before I look away, pulling my phone out to check the time.

"What's so funny?"

My head snaps up at the voice of the man, shocked that he heard me. I turn my head to look behind me because he surely can't be talking to me. But when I see that there's no one else but the two of us, I realize that he is.

He walks closer to me, closing the space between us until he's no more than an arms length away. From this close I have to look up to see his face. I take a moment to take in his features, my eyes darting across his face. Light brown skin, dark, thick eyebrows, and low cut facial hair. His deep brown eyes stare intently at me waiting for my response to a question I don't even really have an answer to. He seems familiar to me even though I'm certain this is the first time we've ever met.

"What's so funny?" he repeats, cocking his head to the side.

That's when I realize why he seems familiar, not because we've met before but instead because it's his face that's on the banners outside the arena for the concert that's set to start in a few hours.

He's Sonny.

Singer. Songwriter. The guy thousands of fans are preparing to watch perform tonight, my best friend included. The realization makes my throat go dry.

"Uh nothing," I finally stammer out, in answer to his question. I motion in the general direction of the exit and start to step around him to leave. "I should probably just uh -"

I feel Sonny's hand on my arm and I stop, turning back to look at him. The warmth of this hand on my skin causes flutters in my stomach. His touch is gentle but firm and though in other circumstances this very action may have felt aggressive, with Sonny it doesn't.

"Nah shorty, you had something to say so let's hear it," Sonny says with amusement in his tone.

His body towers over mine but I don't let our size difference make me feel small. I look him directly in his eyes as I speak.

"You were being an asshole. Which is ridiculous by the way."

"And why is that ridiculous?"

I scoff. "If you don't understand why treating the people who work for you like shit is ridiculous, then you have bigger problems than a fucked up contract. And with all of the money you make

I'm sure you pay him and the rest of your team to do what you want so there's no need to be an asshole about it."

"So you hear one conversation and think you have it all figured out," he says, his tone rough.

"No," I retort. "I think that just because you have money and power it doesn't mean that you get to treat people like shit. All the money in the world doesn't give you a free pass to be an asshole."

He stares at me blankly before his expression morphs into amusement, he throws his head back in laughter. His laugh is deep and warm, echoing through the empty hallway.

When he finishes he looks back down at me, a hint of a smile left on his lips. "You know, I can't remember the last time someone talked to me that way."

If I'm being honest I'm not sure why *I* even spoke to him that way. Not because he didn't deserve to hear it but still I'm just... surprised.

"Maybe that's your problem."

"So you do know who I am."

"Well no, I don't know you," I reply. "But I recognize who you are now, yeah."

Sonny takes a few steps back away from me and I think he's going to leave but instead he crosses his arms over his chest and just looks at me.

"I didn't catch your name," Sonny says after some moments of silence.

"That's because I never said it," I say with a small chuckle.

"Are you here for the show?" He tries again.

"No, I'm actually working tonight."

"Me too."

I crack a smile and roll my eyes. "You're performing in front of a sold out crowd. I'm serving beers and nachos to pay for college before going home and doing homework. Not exactly the same line of work."

"What are you in school for?"

"Marketing."

"That's amazing," Sonny says with a smile. "Are you cold?"

"What?" I ask, confused by the question.

Sonny nods towards my arms. "You have goosebumps."

"Oh yeah, I guess I am," I say, rubbing my hand over my arm. "They keep the arena cold because of all the people."

Sonny reaches over his head and begins to pull his hoodie off. The motion causes a small part of his stomach to be exposed, showing off the muscles and a small trail of hair that leads down to the waistband of his joggers. I avert my eyes and look down at my shoes, not wanting to get caught staring.

"Here take this," he says, holding the hoodie out towards me.

I look at the hoodie and then back to his face, unsure whether he's serious or not. Without the hoodie he's left in just a plain white tee, but even in just the t-shirt and joggers I can't deny that he's attractive.

I open my mouth to decline but Sonny pushes the hoodie towards me again. "C'mon at least let me show you that I'm not always an asshole."

I take the hoodie and hold it in my hands for a second, it's still warm from being on his body. Before I can think too deeply about what it means for this man to have given me his hoodie, I put my arms into the sleeves and pull the hoodie over my head. My nostrils fill with the scent of him, soap and cologne and something else that I can only describe as, man.

He offers me another smile, this one is bigger and reveals dimples in both of his cheeks . "So you're still not gonna give me your name?"

"I'm sure you have more important things to do than stand around talking to a stranger."

"You wouldn't be a stranger if you gave me your name."

"Laila. My name is Laila," I concede.

He sticks a hand out to me. "Hi Laila, I'm Bryce."

I take his hand shaking it. "Bryce?"

I expected him to use Sonny, the name he's widely known as, not something so personal.

The door he came from opens and Bryan sticks his head out. If Bryan has any thoughts about Sonny being out here with a random girl he doesn't let on. "Yo Sonny, we gotta get going."

"I guess I'll see you around Laila," he says, backing up a few steps before turning around and heading towards Bryan. The door closing shut behind the both of them.

I take a second to process all that just happened. I look down at my phone and realize that I'm late.

"Shit."

***

I check one more time to make sure my boss isn't around before I leave from behind the counter of the concessions stand. I am supposed to be cleaning up after the crowds of people ordering concessions before, and during the show, but I want to catch a little bit of the performance. Something we definitely aren't supposed to do, but my coworkers do it anyway on occasion. I slide the black velvet curtain to the side and step into the arena. The arena is packed with people and clouded in a haze from the smoke machines and fireworks that go off around the stage. The combination of the music and crowd is deafening as Sonny performs one of his most popular songs. He's standing in the middle of the stage wearing a White Sox jersey that hangs open showing a white tank underneath. Light wash jeans hang low on his hips and his outfit is completed with the pair of retro Jordan 1s on his feet.

Sonny's stage presence is captivating. I can't bring myself to pull my eyes from him on the stage and I'm sure that everyone else in the building feels the same way. He moves around the stage fluidly and sensually, grasping the microphone in one hand, holding it out to the crowd periodically, encouraging them to sing along with him.

One of the backup dancers stops in front of him and the crowd goes crazy with cheers and applause. She makes a show of bending at the waist and pushing her ass into him and twerking as Sonny smiles and dances with her. I know that most women in this building would give anything to swap places with that dancer, and I would be lying if I said that it didn't stir something within me too. When the song nears its end the music fades out and for a moment all that's left is Sonny's voice as he belts into the microphone and the audience joins in and sings the final words of the song with him.

The arena goes black signaling the end of the concert and the people around me begin to collect their things to leave. I turn around to go back to the concession stand saying a silent prayer hoping that Martin didn't notice my absence. Before I make the few steps to go through the curtain that leads into the hallways the lights come back on to a dim deep blue.

"I would just like one more moment of your time, if you'll allow it."

I stop and turn my focus back to the stage. The crowd immediately begins to go crazy. The cheers intensify when Sonny walks back onto the stage, a stool in his hand as he walks towards the front of the stage. He sets the stool down and sits on it.

"Thank you, thank you, thank you. There aren't enough words for me to be able to thank y'all enough for all that y'all have done for me and the continued support over the years."

Once again the crowd breaks out into cheers and applause. He holds up his free arm and motions for quiet before continuing speaking.

"No seriously, never in a million years did I think, me, a poor kid from the south side of Chicago would be on tour, performing for sold out crowds. I'm living a life that I never thought would be possible for me. But I met someone today who reminded me that none of that matters if you lose sight of who you are. All of the money and the fame in the world mean nothing if you have to give up your integrity to get there. So tonight, I'd like to perform a song that y'all have never heard before, but it's really close to my heart."

He pauses for a moment, turning his head to look at each area of the arena. "And if you're out there and you can hear this song, just know that I heard you."

2
Laila

My feet are killing me. After hours in these heels I am dying to take them off. Thankfully, the pain my feet are suffering through wasn't for nothing. The investor presentation for *Lovely Day*, the Black owned and woman owned beauty company I work for, went phenomenally well and the investors agreed to sign with the company. I spent weeks collecting data and turning it into visuals to show the growth of the company's social media presence, which in turn led to growth in profits, and today it all paid off.

After an exhausting day I would much rather be in my bed binge-watching one of my favorite tv shows, but instead I let Zara talk me into *another* blind date. This time it's the brother of one of her long-time clients. Her argument is always that things can be a fun time even if they aren't meant to be long term. And worst case scenario, it's a story to tell. So far it's been a whole lot of stories to tell and not much else. At this point, I'm not even sure why I keep agreeing to go on these blind dates, but Zara somehow always manages to find a way to convince me. Zara is the person who knows me best in the world, my best friend since elementary school and damn near my sister for all intents and purposes.

I slide into a seat at the bar where we agreed to meet for drinks. When I catch the bartender I order a Cosmopolitan and take a moment to take in my surroundings while I wait for him to make my drink. This hotel bar is significantly more bougie than what I would ever choose for first date drinks but my date had insisted, stating something about their excellent menu options. It is less busy than I expected for this time of night, leaving a lot of the tables surrounding me unoccupied.

My phone buzzes inside my purse, when I pull it out I see that it's a text from Zara.

Zara

> Have fun on your date! I can't wait to hear all about it!

The bartender sets down my drink in front of me and I wonder if it's too late for me to cancel this date. I could always say that something came up at work and I wasn't able to get away and —

"You must be Laila."

On my left a man steps up to the bar. He's shorter than I expected, probably only a couple of inches taller than me and I'm only 5'5 on a good day.

Stop being judgy I internally tell myself, plastering a smile on my face.

"Yes hi, Jason right?"

***

I am officially never letting Zara set me up on a date ever again.

"I really think that if people took the time to understand the market and — "

At that I tune him out, only offering forced polite smiles and nods. For the past hour he's been talking about himself and his job in finance and I couldn't be more bored out of my mind. I tip my martini glass to my lips and drink the last of my second Cosmopolitan. I send a silent thanks to my past self who agreed to drinks rather than dinner because at least the liquor and shorter time commitment is making this experience slightly more bearable.

Jason pauses for a moment and I take the opportunity to try and get away.

"I'm gonna go to the restroom."

"Oh okay, yeah cool," Jason replies, saying the first words in a long time that aren't about himself or his career.

I grab my purse and swiftly make my way away from the bar. I have no idea if I'm even going in the right direction but I put some distance between Jason and I before I stop to ask a waitress for help. She points me to the back of the restaurant, an area tucked away from all the tables. Thankfully, there isn't a line and I am able to walk right into the bathroom.

I don't actually have to use the bathroom, but in the moment it was the first thing to come to mind so that I could have a second to myself to think and breathe and figure out how the hell to nicely leave this terrible date. I have never been one to ditch a date, but leaving this bathroom and this date entirely without another word is an idea I'm seriously considering.

I give myself a moment to stand at the sinks with my eyes closed and take a few deep breaths. After that I stall for a little while longer. I touch up my lip gloss, fluff out my curly hair, scroll through social media, anything to kill time. Finally, I try to reason with myself. The faster I go back out there the faster I can be home in my bed with snacks. With a sigh I grab my purse off the counter. It's time to rip the proverbial Band-Aid off. I yank the door open and step out into the hall, colliding with a hard body. I stumble backwards, losing my balance for a moment until I'm held by my elbows by whoever I bumped into.

"My bad, are you good?" A deep voice asks.

"I'm so sorry I should've been —," my words die on my tongue when I finally look up and see who I've run into, literally.

"Laila?"

Sonny.

"I - um, yes hi," I stutter out. My words fail me as my brain literally tries to catch up to the fact that out of all the people I could have possibly run into, it's Sonny. I would be lying if I said that I never thought about him, or that night ever again, but I figured it was a fluke and there was no way I would ever speak to him again.

"Damn, I never thought I would get the chance to see you again." Sonny says, releasing my elbows but still standing close enough that I'm surrounded by the smell of him and his cologne. My skin misses the warmth of his contact as soon as he lets me go and the cool air sends a slight shiver through my body

I let out a surprised chuckle. "I didn't think you would remember me, it's been years."

"Of course I remember you," he says with the corner of his mouth turning up. "Not many people call me an asshole within the first two minutes of meeting me."

"You deserved it."

A smile takes over Sonny's face. "You're right, I did."

I smile too, and I can't help but feel a sense of deja vu from running into Sonny again like this. Physically he hasn't changed much, but I'm sure like me, a lot has changed with him that can't be seen.

I catch him giving me a once over, his eyes taking me in until his gaze lands on my eyes and he finally speaks.

"So how have you been? What are you doing with that degree of yours?"

Again, I'm shocked that he remembers such an insignificant detail of my life that I told him years ago.

"And what makes you assume I got my degree? Maybe I didn't finish," I say jokingly.

"No disrespect to anyone that decides to leave college," he replies. "But something tells me that when you want something you don't stop til you get it."

I have no rebuttal for that because it's true, I am that way.

"I graduated a few years ago, and now I'm a social media manager for a skin care company."

Sonny gives me a smirk, satisfied with himself that he was right about me.

"And what about you?" I ask. "Are you back from your hiatus?"

"You been keeping tabs on me Laila?"

"What? No, it's just out there," I say quickly waving my hand to try to show that its not a big deal.

Truth is I hadn't been keeping tabs on Sonny, but buzz about him is everywhere. Since his last tour he hasn't made any new music, or done any performances, which is unlike him.

"I know, I'm just fucking with you. I've just been laying low, reevaluating what I want from life."

I nod my head in understanding.

"Aye Sonny, you aight man?"

Like I've been caught doing something I shouldn't, I take a few steps back from Sonny. We hadn't been very close but knowing how innocent situations get turned upside down, I didn't want to take any chances.

"Yeah I'm all good," Sonny says. "I ran into someone on my way from the bathroom, or really she ran into me." Sonny shoots me a mischievous glance before looking back at the other guy.

"Laila, this is Xavier," Sonny says making introductions. "X this is Laila."

Xavier tips his head in my direction in acknowledgement. "Nice to meet you Laila."

"You too Xavier," I reply with a smile.

"They're ready for you upstairs whenever you're good," Xavier says to Sonny.

"Okay just give me a second."

"I have to get back to my table, but it was good to see you," I say.

I'm not necessarily in a hurry to get back to my "date", but more so to give myself some space to process this crazy encounter.

"Are you still here in the city?"

I shake my head. "No, I'm out in Rosewood now."

Rosewood is a city north of Chicago. Historically Black, but for years it was neglected, lacking the necessary resources that help a community thrive. With the help of new businesses and community improvements, Rosewood has grown to be a thriving city. When I graduated from college I had no desire to go back home and with an amazing job offer it was a no brainer for me to stay.

"Let me take you out sometime."

My eyes go wide at Sonny's forward statement.

"I don't think that's a good idea," I reply, shaking my head. "I have a lot going on and I'm not really looking for anything right now."

If he's shocked by me turning him down he doesn't show it. Behind him Xavier tries but fails to hide a laugh behind a cough.

"My bad," Xavier says with another forced cough. "There was something in my throat."

Sonny shoots a look his way before he offers, "How about we exchange Instagrams then? And I can give you my number in case you want to reach out, things on IG can get lost sometimes."

It takes a minute for my brain to understand what he's saying, the shock of running into him again taking over, but when I realize he's serious I dig into my purse to grab my phone. I unlock it and hand it to him with Instagram open. Sonny quickly types in his handle, presses the follow button, then navigates to my contacts and adds his number. His hand brushes mine when he hands my phone back to me, sending a jolt of warmth through my body again.

I need to get away from this man.

"I really do have to go, but it was good to see you." I offer him a smile over my shoulder as I leave.

What the actual fuck.

My steps lead me away from Sonny and back to the bar but my heart is pounding double time. It was a simple conversation yet my entire body is tingling almost as if all of my limbs fell asleep and are taking their sweet time waking back up. Jason accepts my excuse to cut the date short without much push back, not even questioning why I was gone for who knows how long.

I decide to call for a rideshare instead of taking the train home like I usually would. When I am in the car I text Zara to let her know I'm on my way home, and rather than putting my phone away I find myself in my contacts list. I scroll through the list passing 'S' where I expect a new contact to be and instead at the very bottom of the list I see a new contact with a singular sun emoji. I can't stop the small smile from coming to my face, or the flutter that's erupted in my stomach.

3
Sonny

My mama would for sure be chewing my ass out right now for how I'm staring at Laila as she walks away. She'd say I'm acting like I don't have any home training, but I don't care. I can't take my eyes off of her.

Laila.

The sway of her hips as she walks away from me. The bounce of her long curly hair that falls down her back. The way the fabric of the short dress she's wearing hugs her ass and shows off her legs.

There's been more occasions than I would like to admit, where I woke up with a woman and couldn't, for the life of me, remember her name. But this girl. Her name and her face were so deeply etched into my brain that even all these years later I couldn't forget.

"You aight man?" Xavier asks with a serious look on his face. He places the back of his hand on my forehead as if to check my temperature. "You must be sick or something, cause I haven't seen you get curved like that since high school."

At that I scowl and swat his hand away as he erupts into laughter at my expense.

"Nah but forreal who is she?"

"No one" I respond dismissively.

He shoots me a side eye that lets me know he doesn't believe me, but I ignore it making my way out of the hallway.

"C'mon man we got a meeting to get to."

Xavier and I ride the private elevator up to the conference room for my meeting. The doors open to a sizable room with floor to ceiling windows. A large table sits in the middle of the room with chairs all around it. At the head of the table sits my manager, Morgan with her laptop open in front of her.

"Well, well, look who finally decided to grace us with his presence," Morgan says jokingly.

She stands from her chair and I walk over to give her a side hug.

"My bad Mo, we got caught up."

Xavier takes a seat in one of the chairs further away from us and starts scrolling on his phone, not paying me or Morgan any attention.

I lean back against the table, my hands resting beside me as I wait for Morgan to start talking. She picks up her iPad and starts scrolling through her notes.

"Alright then, let's get to business."

I give her a nod in agreement and she begins to walk back and forth in the room, something she does alot during our meetings. Other people could see it as nerves but Morgan and I have worked together for a while now and I know that that is the farthest thing from the truth, movement just helps her work best.

"Essence's people reached out," Morgan says. "They still want you to feature on some songs on her upcoming album."

"No."

"I know you said no before," Morgan continues. "But this could be a great way to slowly get yourself back out there -"

"My answer is no, Morgan."

Morgan halts her steps and looks right at me. "Sonny..."

"Morgan...," I parrot back to her in the same tone she said my name in.

Morgan glares at me, clearly annoyed that I have shot this opportunity down again.

"I know what you're thinking, Mo."

"Do you know what I'm thinking?" She asks, raising an eyebrow. "Because for months now we've talked about what you want to do next and it has *always* included music, but now I'm not so sure. And if you don't, that's fine, we can pivot and focus on different aspects of your career but you can't keep me in the dark, Sonny."

I push off from the table and walk closer to the windows, shoving my hands into my pockets. The sun has gone down but the city is alive beneath us. The brake lights and street lights illuminate the darkness and people hustle to their next destination.

"I'm not giving up on music," I reply, my eyes still focused on the city below us.

I could never give up on music. Truthfully it was never music that I left. It was everything else that I needed a break from, the politics and business of it all. But music, I couldn't give that up even if I tried. I've been writing songs since I was 14 and a lot of the time it's not something I have to sit down and try to do, it just happens and I listen.

"So what's your plan then? You wanted a break from everything and I understand that. I agreed even. But now you've left me in the dark."

Instead of answering Morgan's question, I ask her one of my own. "Morgan, do you remember why I said 'yes' to you being my manager?"

Shortly after my last tour ended, I left the label that I had been signed to since the beginning of my career. It was time for me to sign a new contract and negotiations had been going back and forth, back and forth, and I knew I needed time away from it all. The shitty deal they wanted me to agree to was very easy to walk away from. I left the label, fired my agent and my manager and was prepared to just *be* for a while. And I did, I did whatever the fuck I wanted for months until I was ready to start taking meetings again.

It was months of taking meetings with different labels and management teams before I met Morgan. She was an assistant to some big shot who came into the meeting with an air of arrogance and making big promises I knew he could never keep.

"Yes of course I remember, Sonny," Morgan replies. "I told you that the song you performed at the end of the Chicago tour date was the best one you've ever made. You asked me why and I said that it felt more personal, more like the real you and not the version of you that you had been giving to the world. And you said that I was the first person that had ever said that, that everyone else said that you should stick to the music you had been making before."

I told the man that there was no way I would work with him, but Morgan... I knew Morgan just needed someone to give her a chance to flourish.

I turn to face Morgan. "Exactly."

"Exactly?" She asks, shaking her head. "I don't follow."

"You were the first person in the industry that said that to me. That's why I wanted to work with you, because you understood what that song meant to me," I pause, taking in a deep breath. "I want to make music for me, music that speaks to me. Not the hypersexual, fame and money bullshit I was forced to push before."

"And I understand that, you know I do but working with Essence can be the first step to that," Morgan says. "Allow you to come back slowly before diving in."

I shake my head. "No. I want to do it on my own, on my own terms."

Morgan stares at my face. I'm not sure what she's trying to see but she must find it because she looks back down at her iPad and continues on with the next thing on her agenda for us to discuss. We continue on, talking through each item on Morgan's list until we reach the real thing that brought me back to Chicago to begin with.

"Have you talked with Tristan about Oasis?" Morgan asks.

"Yeah we talked before I got on the plane today. He said that everything went as expected, we have all the inspections done and the liquor license. The contractors are finishing up the last few things, but we're still set to open in two weeks."

"Perfect," Morgan replies, scribbling notes into her iPad. "I'll coordinate with his assistant about all the finer details."

I nod in agreement.

"Aye y'all almost done over there? A nigga gettin hungry," Xavier says from the other end of the table.

Morgan and I both burst out laughing at Xavier's interruption. X loves him some food and is always down for a meal.

"You can't go two hours without food Xavier," Morgan says, rolling her eyes.

Xavier dramatically rubs his belly and grins at her. "I'm a big boy Morgan."

Morgan rolls her eyes again and picks up her bag to pack up her things. "I don't have anything else to discuss, I have your flight set for after the opening of Oasis but let me know if you want to change the date to spend more time with your family."

"I don't think I'm going back to LA."

Morgan pauses packing her bag and looks up at me. "So you really just came here to make my life difficult today, huh?"

I crack a smile at her comment. "Nah never that, Mo. I haven't spent more than a few days or weeks here since I was 19. Maybe it's time for me to come home."

"And when did you decide this?"

"Right now," I reply with a sheepish smile.

Morgan picks up her phone and starts typing away. "Okay, I will cancel your flight but I'm assuming you would need to go back at least once to get some of your stuff. And I will also get started on finding you a long term rental."

"Thank you, Mo. You're a lifesaver."

"Mmhmm," she replies, waving me off. "Just remember all the life saving I do when you wanna swipe that black card on something. I like handbags and I wear a size 8."

We both laugh but I silently make a note in my head to send her something nice once all of this is done. Morgan takes good care of me so I don't mind going the extra mile for her.

4
Laila

I ONLY MAKE IT a few steps into the loft before I pull off my heels and leave them right there by the front door. I hang my purse on the hook and pad into the kitchen, turning on lights as I go since Zara isn't home yet. Zara and I have lived together since we were freshmen in college, first in the dorms and then in some really shitty off campus apartments. Now we live in a gorgeous loft that has everything we were looking for: modern updates, open floor plan, close to the train, and floor to ceiling windows with a pretty view.

In my room, I take off the clothes I wore to work in favor of something more comfortable. I pull on a pair of pajama pants and go into my closet in search of a hoodie. With work being so busy, I haven't kept up with laundry so a lot of the hangers are empty. I shuffle through my remaining hoodies until my eyes land on the one that's been in the back of my closet unworn for the past three years. Impulsively, I slide the hoodie off the velvet hanger and pull it over my head to put it on. It doesn't smell like him anymore but the buttery softness of the fabric is still the same.

I'm not sure why I even kept it for so long since seeing Sonny again was never something I even thought would happen. Hell, seeing Sonny the first time was something that wasn't supposed to have happened.

My stomach grumbles, bringing me out of my thoughts and reminding me that I haven't eaten since the late lunch I took at work. I leave my bedroom and go to the kitchen in search of food. I take a quick glance through the fridge and cabinets and come up empty for anything that wouldn't require way more effort than I'm willing to put in right now.

Looks like I'm definitely ordering something.

I grab a handful of Oreos to snack on as I lean against the counter and scroll through my food delivery apps. Tacos from a local restaurant is ultimately what I decide on and I start to place my order when I hear the jingling of Zara's keys at our front door.

"Heyyy!" Zara calls out as she walks into the kitchen.

"Hey I'm about to order tacos," I reply. Do you want something?"

"Ooooo yes," Zara replies. "Steak tacos and a large horchata please. I'm starving."

I add what Zara asked for to my order and schedule it for delivery.

"Did you have a late client tonight?"

Zara leaves the kitchen and heads to her room but because of the open space of the loft I can still hear her when she replies. "Yeah, one of my regulars needed a later appointment, which was fine, but I had back to back clients all day and barely had time to sit down or eat."

Zara is a barber and hair stylist, one of the best, so her books are always filled up weeks in advance. A few minutes later Zara comes back changed out of the black cargo pants and cropped shirt she was in and into a sports bra and pajama shorts.

Zara sits down on the couch and wraps one of the blankets we leave laying on it, around herself.

"Soo since you're home so early I guess it didn't go well?" Zara asks.

I join Zara on the couch. "It's not even that early, it's like 8 o'clock."

"Yeah, but if it would have gone well then drinks would have led to more and you wouldn't be sitting there side eyeing me," Zara replies with a laugh.

"You would be side eyeing too if you had to endure spending time with that man!"

"Girl it could not have been that bad."

"Z, he talked for an hour about the stock market and how everyone needs a Roth IRA. Don't get me wrong I know the importance of savings and all that, but I was not prepared to have an in depth conversation about it on a first date. Instead of 'how was your day' it was all 'so what does your investment portfolio look like?'."

Zara cringes. "I swear he seemed nice and normal when I met him."

"Yeah well that's going to be my first and last date with Jason," I reply. "And I'm not going out with anyone else you set me up with either. No more coworker's baby mama's second cousin twice removed, or whoever the hell they are."

My exaggeration makes Zara laugh but I am so serious. I'm so over dealing with men right now.

When our takeout comes Zara answers the door to retrieve it and we sit on the couch eating our food and rewatching one of our favorite shows until way too late at night.

***

If I never had to see snow again I'd be a happy woman. That statement is so dramatic, especially since I have lived with snowy winters my entire life and should be used to it by now. But the half a foot of snow that accumulated overnight has brought out the drama. The hassle that snow brings to life never feels worth it, even if it is beautiful to look at when it's pristine and untouched.

I would have opted for a work from home day but since I was in meetings all day yesterday I wasn't able to finish all of the things I needed to. So here I am trudging through the cold and snow after waiting on a delayed train, until I finally reach the *Lovely Day* office.

I interned at *Lovely Day* my senior year of college as a part of my graduation requirements, but I fell in love with the business. So much so that after graduation when Cassandra, the owner, offered me a full time marketing position I jumped at the opportunity.

Attending the nearby university introduced me to Rosewood and once I was here I fell in love. Rosewood is a suburban city bordering Chicago and Lake Michigan. Decades ago it was in a state of desolation, lacking necessary care and funding after many people left the area for other places. Rosewood is a place built by the Black community, for the Black community. Long time residents banded together, pouring time, money and resources to help Rosewood become a thriving town again. They laid the foundation for the flourishing Black community that it is today. Even though Rosewood is not a small town, it is very close knit.

I use my keyfob to get into the building, stomping off the extra snow stuck to my snow boots as I walk in and take the elevator up to the office. The office consists of Cassandra's personal office, a large open space where we all usually sit to work or have meetings, a small kitchen and the warehouse where we store all of our product inventory.

I change out of my snow boots and into a pair of sneakers I brought with me in my bag and walk over to the conference table to get ready for our morning meeting. Cass is already there, as usual, typing away on her computer. I sit in my usual spot at the table and pull out my iPad and laptop.

"Good morning."

"Hey, good morning," Cass replies with a smile. "Stella is here and Reagan said she's on her way and will be here in a few."

"Okay, sounds good."

Though *Lovely Day* has grown, we are still very much a small operation of just four women. Cass works as CEO and handles all of the overhead. I focus on social media and marketing. Stella and Reagan are in charge of operations and handle the ins and outs of shipping and inventory. There are things that we outsource, but for the most part it's all us.

When everyone is settled, Cass starts off the morning meeting. She gives an overall debrief and then each of us have a chance to talk about what we have been working on individually.

"We have almost all of the inventory we were waiting on for the new collection," Reagan says. "There's just one more pallet but it's supposed to be delivered tomorrow and another that's being delivered next week."

"Laila, when are you doing the product pictures?" Cass asks.

"I'm going to take some teaser pictures of the new products today, but I have a full photoshoot scheduled for next week."

"Okay, that should work perfectly."

The meeting continues with everyone talking about what we have going on and the plans that we have coming up for *Lovely*

Day. Once everything is discussed Cass tells us that she has one more thing that she wants to talk about.

"So as we all know, Laila did a great job with the investors yesterday and they agreed to give us what we were asking for," Cass says. "With that funding, things are looking good for the possibility of expansion this year."

My eyes go wide with surprise, I had always known that Cass wanted *Lovely Day* to grow into something more, but I didn't realize how real of a possibility it was becoming. "Wait really?"

Cass nods and shifts her long knotless braids over her shoulder. "We would need our sales to keep being consistent, but if all goes well then new products and more inventory and maybe even more staff, can all be a reality. And of course a bigger space because we're already bursting at the seams here."

"That's amazing!" Reagan replies.

"Nothing's set in stone, I haven't even gone to look at locations yet. But it is something that is very real for this new year."

"Let's make it happen then," Stella says with determination in her voice.

The morning meeting ends and we all break off to work on our own things. I go into the warehouse to pick out some of the new products and then spend the rest of my morning and into the afternoon taking pictures and handling messages and comments on our social media.

We place an order for lunch from a restaurant down the street and Stella goes to get it for us. After lunch Cass comes out from her office to tell us she's leaving for the day.

"Since tomorrow is Friday, I'm going to work from home," Cassandra says.

"Because it's Friday or because Cyrus is back from a trip?" Stella jokes.

"She wants to go see her man," Reagan says in a sing-song voice.

If her brown skin would have allowed it, Cass would be red in the face from our teasing. A little over a year ago Cass went on a solo trip to Mexico and came back with a fine ass boyfriend, some straight out of a romance movie shit. Cyrus is a pilot and they were long distance for over a year and then he moved here to Rosewood for her. It surprised the hell out of all of us because Cass and spontaneous don't usually go together, but Cyrus brings out something in her that gives her the safety to be impulsive.

"I hate all of you," Cass says laughing.

"Notice how she couldn't even deny it," Reagan chimes in and we all laugh.

"Yeah, yeah whatever. I'll see y'all on Monday," Cass replies, raising her hand in goodbye.

I stay a little bit longer and work on editing the pictures I took earlier in the day and planning out posts for all our social media accounts. I turn up the music in my headphones and get lost in work. By the time I look up again, the sun has set and my eyes burn from staring at a screen so long.

Shit.

I didn't mean to lose track of time like that. I close my laptop and pack my things to leave. I put my snow boots and coat back on and head out of the office, locking the door behind me. As I step off the elevator and out into the cold night air my phone starts to ring. I pull it out of my pocket and check to see who it is.

Mom

With a sigh, I swipe my finger across the screen to answer the call as I walk to the train station. "Hello?"

"You don't know how to pick up a phone and call your mother anymore?"

I let out a long sigh. "I've had a lot going on mom, I wasn't doing it on purpose."

"Well I was just calling to check in on you. How are you doing?"

"I'm doing good. I'm on my way home from work right now."

"That's good to hear," my mom replies.

The line goes silent for a few moments as I wait for her to say the real reason why she's calling me. I know my mother and unfortunately for me I also know that these calls are never just a casual check in.

"Listen, I need to borrow some money until next week, just for some necessities."

And there it is. I roll my eyes, frustrated but not surprised because I can't remember the last time my mom called me and didn't ask me for something.

"What happened to the money that I just gave you a few weeks ago?"

"I told you my car was in the shop and I needed some help with the repairs."

She had said that. And the time before that it was groceries and the time before that it was because the washing machine was broken. It's always something.

I make it to my train station and walk down the stairs. I pull my card from my coat pocket and tap it on the scanner to unlock the turnstiles.

"How much do you need?" I ask flatly.

"Just a hundred dollars. Money is a little tight right now and I -"

I don't bother to listen to the rest of her sentences. Instead I pull the phone away from my face and open my online banking app. I type in the amount that she asked for and press the button to send the money to her.

"I sent it but I gotta go, my train is here."

It wasn't, but now that she said the real reason she called me, there was nothing else I needed to say to my mom.

"Okay thank you, I love you," she replies sweetly.

I end the call, close my eyes and take a few deep breaths. The automated voice on the intercom alerts of a train approaching. I take three more deep breaths and open my eyes to my train slowly riding into the station until it finally stops and the doors open. I step onto the train and opt to stand instead of sitting between people. The train is decently full but since I worked later than I meant to, I missed the evening rush. The automated voice comes over the intercom again to alert that the doors are closing. A few seconds later, the doors close and the train pulls away from the station with a jolt.

All of the exhaustion of working all day hits me on my commute home. I eat dinner and then head to my bathroom to take a shower. The hot droplets of water hitting my skin as I step into the shower feel heavenly. So much so that for a while I just stand there and enjoy the warmth and calm that the water pouring off of my skin brings. After my shower I put on some pajamas and get into bed. I turn on my tv and set the volume low to act as background noise while I'm awake and to help me fall asleep. Though tonight is a night that I know sleep won't evade me because my eyes are already heavy while I open Instagram to do my nighttime scroll.

Stories is where I usually start scrolling, and once I get bored of that I switch to the actual timeline to see the posts of the people I follow. I scroll aimlessly until one post in particular catches my eye, or rather less the post and more who posted it. It's a picture of the city at night, darkness in direct contrast with the lights of buildings and cars and clearly captured from many stories above the ground and a simple caption that just says 'home'.

Sonny followed me back on Instagram the day after we ran into each other and liked the most recent picture that I had posted. With everything going on with life and work I haven't thought much about him and I haven't even told Zara about running into him again. Hesitantly, I click on his handle to go to his profile. He doesn't post often, once a month at most but frequently less often than that. A throwback picture of toddler Sonny with his mom that he posted for Mother's Day a few years ago, brings a smile to my face. His mother is stunning and Sonny is in her arms with one of those big cheesy grins that kids make when they're really happy. My eyes have gotten heavier and slowly without me noticing I slip into slumber, my phone falling onto the bed next to me.

5
Sonny

Stepping away from performing and releasing music for the first time, since I was signed to a record label at 19, made it blatant that I needed to diversify my financial portfolio. Not that I hadn't been before, but I wanted to do more than I had been previously. Because whether it was now or some time in the future, there would come a time when I wanted to step away from music for good and I needed to be prepared for that. Over the years I had invested in some different avenues and I prided myself on saving far more money than I spent, but I wanted to continue to live a comfortable life.

The desire to move into other business ventures is how I met Tristan Hawthorne. Tristan's family has deep ties to the construction and real estate industries and have been prominent in it for generations. When it got back to Tristan that I was interested in partnering together he was open to the idea and thus our partnership on Oasis began.

Tristan is standing by the bar in the middle of Oasis when I walk in through the back entrance. There are very few times when I've met with Tristan and he hasn't been in a perfectly tailored suit, so I figured today would be no different and I was right. He's wearing a black button down shirt and navy dress pants, the matching suit jacket resting on the bar stool next to him and black loafers. His back is to me and he's on the phone, cursing somebody out by the sounds of it.

The phone call ends as I walk up next to Tristan at the bar.

"My bad about that," Tristan says, hanging up the phone.

"No worries, everything alright?"

"Yeah it is now. Half of my liquor order was missing so I had to get into it with my distributor because that shit is unacceptable."

I nod in agreement. "Glad that it got straightened out."

"Yeah there was no question about it if they wanted to keep my business."

The door to one of the storage rooms opens and a man wearing a beanie and white shirt emerges pushing a dolly with cases of liquor on it.

When he nears us he nods his head to me and Tristan. "What's up, boss."

"The rest of that order should be here by the end of the day. And I need you to do another inventory check to make sure everything is good for the opening."

"Got it, I'll handle it after I get everything stocked up."

Tristan nods and then looks over at me. "Sonny, this is one of the bar managers, Rico."

I hold out my fist to Rico and he bumps mine with his own. "Good to meet you Rico."

"You too," Rico replies with a nod and then starts to unload the bottles from the dolly.

"Let me show you around," Tristan says.

The last time I was here to see the space in person had been right after the drywall had been installed, very much still in the thick of construction. To say that it looks completely different is an understatement. When Tristan first showed me the location it was just an empty building in an area of Rosewood that had previously had a lot of warehouses and storage spaces that were now transitioning to being used for new ventures. I have seen the space go from an empty warehouse, to new framing and walls, to drywall and flooring to now.

We walk through the whole building, from the main floor and upstairs to the bathrooms and the stock rooms, Tristan shows me everything, which I appreciate. I wanted my investment in Oasis to be more than money. The money was absolutely a factor, but I wanted to have more involvement in it and make sure that it was something I was proud to be a part of.

Now, it's a beautiful two story lounge. The main bar sits directly in the middle of the first floor, a perfect square with space for bartenders to work each of the four sides. Booths line the perimeter of the room and couches, loveseats and accent chairs fill in the rest of the space with small side tables as well.

The interior designers went for a moody aesthetic, the main colors of the space being blacks and greens with pops of gold throughout. The DJ booth is in the far back corner across from the stairs to go up to the second floor. The second floor is exclusive to members of Oasis only, those who pay a premium for a more secluded space. The upper level has a balcony that allows you to see from upstairs to the lower level below.

"So," Tristan says, gesturing out to the room. "What do you think of the place?"

"It's come a long way and it looks fantastic. Your team did a great job."

"I had no doubt that they would," he replies. "But it's still amazing to see it come to life."

I nod in agreement and decide then that this won't be the last time that I invest in a project like this. Watching the journey of building Oasis feels like the start of a whole new venture for me.

Tristan and I say our goodbyes and go our separate ways. I leave through the back door and go back to my car where Xavier is waiting for me. Xavier is my friend, but he's also my right hand man, an extra set of eyes and ears to keep me safe. I hired him officially to be my bodyguard shortly after I became well known enough to need one. A lot of the time wherever I go, X goes too. He stayed in the car for this meeting with Tristan because I knew it wouldn't take long and I wasn't worried about any trouble.

Xavier is in the driver's seat and I slide into the passenger seat of the blacked out SUV.

"All good?" Xavier asks.

"Yeah I'm good."

Xavier puts the car in drive and pulls out of the parking spot and I relax back in my seat, getting comfortable for the drive ahead of us.

One of the things about X that I appreciate the most, is that he never feels the need to fill the natural silence that falls between us, he just lets it be. He's playing music from his phone that's connected to the car, but neither of us feels the need to fill the space with filler conversation. The silence is comfortable and speaks to X's chill demeanor, but also the familiarity between us because we were friends way before me 'making it big' was anything more than something I daydreamed about instead of paying attention in math class. And even now, when my life has changed drastically, X has remained solid, never switching up on me unlike a lot of other people who I thought were my friends but didn't have good intentions. The ones who saw our relationship as transactional and were only looking for what I could do for them instead of caring about me as a person.

My phone buzzes and I reach into my pocket to grab it. It's a picture from Morgan of the orange Louis Vuitton shopping bag and the purse I had delivered to her, sitting on her desk. The simple words, 'I could get used to this' follow the picture.

Morgan handled a lot of the details of my transition from living in LA to Chicago. Within two days of me telling her that I wanted to move back here, she had tours of condos set up for me to go view, transport for my cars established and a bunch of other things that I hadn't even thought of needing to do, done for me. Though she had been joking about me buying her shoes or a handbag, I actually did want to buy something for her as a thank you.

After I reply to Morgan with a laughing emoji, I close out of my messages and open Instagram instead to pass the time during this drive. I scroll for a little while, dropping a few likes on my friends' pictures until I get bored. Before I leave the app I tap on my notifications. Something about the little icon next to the notifications always bothers me and I have to open it any time I'm on the app to clear it. Thankfully, I have it set to only notify me when someone I follow back has interacted so the amount of notifications I receive is drastically less than what it could be. I do a few quick swipes through the notifications, most of them for the last few things that I have posted until I see one that isn't. A picture that I posted was liked 16 hours ago by withlove.laila. A smirk crosses my face knowing that there was absolutely no way she liked that picture intentionally. It had been over a week since I ran into Laila and though we had exchanged social media and I had given her my number, she hadn't reached out. I had been following her lead on not communicating because though I wanted to, I wanted to respect her space especially since she was so hesitant to share information in the first place. However, this was a golden opportunity dropped straight into my lap, I wasn't gonna pass it up.

I take a screenshot of the notification list and crop the picture until it shows just the one and tap on Laila's name to go to her profile. Her page is perfectly curated, a mix of pictures of her alone or with friends, one girl in particular showing up more than others, and pictures of the world. Sunsets and the lake and flowers amongst other things that somehow all go together perfectly. I go to her messages, type out my message, and hit send before I can think too much about it.

sonny

you stalking me laila?

My hands are clammy, actually my whole body is warm. I set my phone down and pull on the collar of my shirt trying to get some reprieve from the sudden influx of heat in my body. When the hell had it gotten so hot in here? Heat pours from the vents of the car and I decide that that must be the cause. I reach over and turn the dial that controls the heat to my side of the car down. I pick my phone up again and see that she's replied.

withlove.laila

no. what makes you think that?

I send her the screenshot of the notification.

sonny

you have to go pretty far down my page to find this gem

The bubbles that indicate she's typing appear then disappear and reappear again. Finally a message from her pops up.

withlove.laila

it's a nice picture. your mom is beautiful.

Her response catches me off guard and makes me laugh, leaving an amused grin in its wake when I'm done. X glances my way but just shakes his head and keeps driving.

sonny

you're right, she is.

sonny

what are you up to today? other than stalking me?

I wait in anticipation for the little bubbles to reappear to indicate that she's responding, but minutes pass by and they don't. The GPS shows that we only have about 20 minutes left for our drive. I close Instagram and open my notes app. Last night I couldn't sleep and as usual when I'm up too late, song lyrics found their way to me. I look at what I have written and it's bare bones, just a part of the chorus and a verse so I spend some time going over it, adding things, taking things out, until I like the direction that it's going.

***

Xavier rolls down his window and leans over to type in the code to the gate. The wrought iron gates slowly slide open to grant us access into the community. The weather has warmed slightly in the past few days, so the nice white snow that blanketed the ground has turned into muddy slush. Xavier pulls into the driveway of my mom's house and kills the engine. I use my key to let us into the side door and almost immediately a little body flings themselves at my legs.

"Uncle Bryce!"

My nephew RJ's arms are wrapped around my leg and he looks up at me, grinning. I reach down and pick him up and give him a big hug.

"What's up little man?" X says. X holds out his hand and RJ gives him an enthusiastic high five.

I set RJ back down and he runs off. Xavier and I take off our shoes and leave them by the door as I head further into the house in search of my mom.

My mom stands in the kitchen, one hand on her hip the other stirring something in a pot on the stove.

"Hey ma," I call out.

She turns and smiles when she sees me and Xavier. I walk into the kitchen and she leaves the stove to give me a hug.

She hugs Xavier too. "How's your mama doing?"

"She's doing good, I'll let her know you asked about her," Xavier replies.

Xavier leaves the kitchen and goes to sit down on the couch in the family room where RJ is playing with a train set. RJ picks up one of the trains and hands it to X to get him to play with him.

"I didn't think you'd be here until a little later."

"My meeting wrapped up a little early so I just decided to come now. Is that okay?"

She stops stirring the pot and turns to give me one of her 'mom' looks. "You have never had to ask permission to be home and you don't need to start now."

My mom walks to the fridge and opens it, pulling out more ingredients for whatever she's making.

"Do you need any help?"

"Nope I got it, but thank you for asking."

I pull out one of the barstools at the island and sit down to spend time with my mom while she cooks.

"Are Lauryn and Shannon here too or just RJ?" I ask in reference to my older sisters.

"No, but they'll be here in a little while. RJ's preschool was closed today so Lauryn asked me to pick him up."

My mom places a cutting board down on the island and starts to cut some of the vegetables that she pulled from the fridge. "How are you doing? How long are you in town for?"

"A while," I reply with a pause. "I've decided to come back to the city."

"Really? That's unexpected."

"Yeah for me too actually," I reply.

"What made you make that decision?"

"I don't know, I came for a short visit a little while ago and it just felt like the right thing. It's not that big of a deal though."

The knife stills, breaking from the rhythmic chops that were happening just seconds before, and my mom looks up from the vegetables to me. She gives me one of those 'mom looks' , the one with the raised eyebrow that says so much without actually saying anything at all.

"What?"

"Nothing," she replies nonchalantly. "I was just seeing if that's the story you're sticking to."

"It's not a big deal, I don't want to make it more than it is."

"Honey, you have been off in Los Angeles ever since you got that deal and started your music career. And you have never once wanted to move back home. You may not want to see it now, but it means something."

I don't have a response to that so instead I shift the conversation to something else for us to talk about while she cooks.

My parents were older when they had me, years after they had had both of my sisters. So between two full fledged careers and everything that comes with taking care of three kids, to say they were busy was an understatement. But a time that I always valued with my mom was when she was cooking. Usually my sisters were out doing an extracurricular activity or with their friends or when I got a little older, away at college. So this was time that I got to spend with just me and my mom.

A while later my sisters Lauryn and Shannon walk in through the front door carrying grocery bags. I stand to greet them and take the bags from their hands.

"B! I'm so happy you're home," Lauryn says, wrapping me in a tight hug.

Lauryn and Shannon have been mistaken for twins for forever even though they are almost two years apart. They both take after our mother, sharing the same umber skin tone and almond eyes while I looked more like our dad.

"It's good to see you too sis."

We all walk together to the kitchen and I set the bags down on the counter.

"Hey girls," Mom says, giving them both kisses on the cheek when they enter the kitchen.

"The store was out of the croutons that you wanted, but we got everything else that you asked for," Shannon says as she starts taking things out of the grocery bags.

"That's okay, the salad will be just fine without them. Where's my son in law, I thought he was coming with you?"

"Ryan was called in for surgery," Lauryn says.

"Okay, I'll make sure to send you home with some food for him."

My mom sets two baking dishes down in front of me, one with lasagna and the other with garlic bread, my favorite meal.

"Set these on the table please. I just have to make something for RJ to eat."

I do as my mom asked while she goes into her pantry and comes back with a cup of microwave mac and cheese. She adds water to it and puts it in the microwave to cook.

"Wow, Ma you're going soft on me," I say, jokingly "We didn't get any special meals. What happened to having to eat what you put on our plate?"

"You only had to eat things you didn't like that one time and I never made them for you again. Don't exaggerate."

The microwave beeps and she takes the cup out and stirs in the powdered cheese that it came with.

"And me and your father didn't do everything a hundred percent right all the time. You just have to do your best and hope your kids turn out okay."

There's a sadness that comes over her voice when she talks about my dad, evidence of the hurt and grief that still fills her body. I step closer and wrap my arm around her shoulders.

"Y'all did great. Even if I am still haunted by peas."

She chuckles and elbows me in the side. "Go wash your hands so we can eat."

I wash my hands in the powder bathroom right off the kitchen. As I walk back I take out my phone just to make sure I haven't missed any important messages. A smile comes to my face when I see the one at the very top.

withlove.laila

> at work. i've been doing a photoshoot all day so no time for stalking (:

6
Laila

"WHAT ARE YOU OVER there smiling about?" Zara asks, standing in the doorway to my room.

"Nothing," I reply quickly.

I close the message that I had been reading from Sonny and look at Zara. I can tell by the look on her face that she doesn't believe me, but she lets me have it and doesn't push for more information. Sonny and I have been talking back and forth for a few days now. There are often long stretches in between replies and we've moved from DMs to texting directly but it's been consistent. But talking to him hasn't been something that I'm ready to share with anyone quite yet.

Zara knows about the first time I ran into Sonny, I spilled everything to her in our college apartment over greasy burgers and fries when we both got home after the concert. We speculated and analyzed every little thing that I could remember about the interaction, but ultimately I decided to chalk it up to just a random run in and go on about my life. And that had been going just fine for me, until I ran into him again.

The odds of me running into Sonny the first time? Dismal. The odds of me running into Sonny again and him wanting to exchange information that subsequently leads to us talking back and forth for days? It should be nonexistent, but here the fuck I am. I haven't told her anything about what's happened recently between me and Sonny.

Me and Sonny?

No.

There is no *me and Sonny.*

I haven't told her about running into Sonny and talking to him, mainly because I know that she'll put more weight into it than I want to at this moment. She'll see it as a sign, some sort of divine intervention bringing us together or something, and I just don't want that right now. I don't have time for that right now and it's only been a few months since... Devin.

I inwardly cringe at even the thought of him and decide to push all those thoughts away and instead focus on Zara.

"A better question is what kept you out all night, hmm?" I ask, turning the attention back on her instead of me.

"Nolan came to see me at the shop and we went back to his place."

"Is that the chef?"

"Nooo," Zara replies, shaking her head. "That's Aaron, Nolan is the surgeon. The one I went to San Diego with last summer."

"Ohhh right, I forgot about him."

Zara's roster of men is always impeccable. She makes it very clear that she doesn't want anything serious, that they will never be "boyfriend and girlfriend" and that she's just there for a good time. And every so often guys will fall off the roster leaving space for a new man. It's truly amazing to see in person and I love it for her because she's totally content with it.

"What are your plans for the day?" Zara asks.

I take an Oreo out of the package that's sitting next to me in my bed and use it to gesture to the TV. "You're looking at it."

"Orrrr," Zara starts.

I groan, knowing that whatever Zara is about to say involves real clothes and leaving this apartment.

"We could go out."

"Or we could not and I can keep watching my show," I reply.

"Please, it'll be fun! And we haven't gone out together in forever."

"You know what's also fun, staying warm in my bed and watching my show."

"Ha ha," Zara replies, sarcastically. "This is like your fiftieth rewatch of this show, it will be here tomorrow."

"Where do you even want to go?"

"Tristan invited me to the soft opening of his lounge tonight and told me to bring a friend."

I lay back against my pillows and sigh. "I don't even have anything to wear."

"Liar, I can think of at least four outfits that you can wear. So next excuse."

Zara looks at me with raised eyebrows and crosses her arms, waiting for my next rebuttal. But I don't have one because she's right, we haven't gone out together in a while. I have been so wrapped up with work and then the holidays and more work *because* of the holidays. Maybe a night out is what I need.

"Fine, I'll go."

"Perfect!"

Zara climbs out of my bed and goes over to my closet, shuffling through my hangers.

"What are we thinking? Skirt? Dress? Oooo this is cute."

Zara holds up a silver mini dress.

"If you're forcing me to go out, I at least want to wear pants. It's cold as hell outside."

"Force is such a negative word," Z replies. "I'm helping you get out of the house to have some fun."

Zara keeps going through my clothes until she pulls out another hanger with a pair of black leather pants that I've never worn. She takes them off the hanger and tosses them on the bed next to me. "Here, pants."

I groan again because I really don't want to go but I stand up, leaving the warmth and coziness of my bed behind. I walk to my bathroom, turning on the light as I enter. My hair has been pulled up into a bun on the top of my head all day. I pull the scrunchie from my hair and let my curls fall loose down my back.

Zara's bathroom has always been our unofficial get ready together place so I grab my makeup bag and hair products to go in there. When we moved into this place, we decided she could have the primary bedroom and ensuite so her bathroom is slightly bigger with way more counter space. Zara follows me into the bathroom and connects her phone to the speaker, selecting a playlist to hype us up while we do our hair and makeup.

Getting ready does lift my mood. Singing along to songs I love with my best friend while making myself feel pretty will always do it for me. Even when my eyeliner decides to look like cousins on their daddy's side instead of sisters. With one last swipe of lip gloss, I step back from the mirror satisfied with my look. My makeup is light, mainly concealer and a soft eyeshadow look. My curls are refreshed and I just leave my hair down. It's been a few days since wash day so I have all the volume but I'm not mad at it. I pack my things back up to take them back to my own room. Zara is still working on her hair, adding more gel to try to get her short, platinum blonde hair to lay flat in finger waves. She bleached it our freshman year of college and has been platinum blonde ever since, a color that suits her well.

In my room, I put all my products away and change into my outfit for the night. I do wear the leather pants and pair it with a white corset top and strappy heels that I will for sure regret by the end of the night. I walk out of my room and see Zara pulling out two shot glasses to go along with the bottle of liquor from our bar cart that she's already placed on the counter. In college, Zara and I would always pregame with at least one shot, a ritual that we have continued on even now.

She pours up for both of us and slides mine towards me. We raise our glasses to each other, clinking them together before we down them, the burn of the alcohol causing me to cringe as it goes down.

Zara puts her heels on and while we wait for the ride share we ordered we take pictures together. Some on our phones and some with my polaroid until we're both satisfied. My phone pings with the notification that our driver is approaching.

"One more for the road?" Zara asks, eyebrows raised.

Fuck it, why not.

I pick up my abandoned shot glass for her to fill up again.

"Yesss," Zara replies, pouring us up again.

We take the shots quickly and then grab our things to head out the door.

***

There's a small line outside of Oasis when we step out of our rideshare but Zara doesn't pay it any mind and walks directly up to security at the door and I follow behind her. I can hear some slight mumbles from some upset people in line but I don't pay them any mind. The guy at the door hands IDs back to two girls and steps aside to let them in the building and then turns his attention to us.

"Zara, you know you're supposed to wait in line like everybody else," the man says, his voice gruff and a little annoyed.

"And why would I do that when I'm not like everybody else?"

"Your ass stay trying to get me in trouble. Go ahead," he replies, motioning towards the door.

"Thank you," Zara says with a sweet smile.

The lights are down low inside Oasis and there's a slight haze in the air. It's busy with people at the bar and others sitting in the various seats around the space, but I can tell it's only a fraction of what it will be on future Saturday nights.

"You want to do a lap to find seats and then I'll get us drinks?" Zara yells over the music, into my ear.

I nod my head and she takes my hand, leading me so we don't get separated. We weave through the tables around people standing and talking until we find an open loveseat near the back of the room.

"What do you want?" Zara asks.

"Just get me whatever you're having," I reply, sitting down in the middle of the seat so no one will sit next to me while Zara is gone.

She nods before she turns on her heel to go to the bar.

I relax back into my seat and take in the space and people around me. The music is louder than background noise but it doesn't stop people from talking with each other. Stepping close to speak into each other's ear or just talking louder to be heard over the music.

"I'm glad she got you to come out."

I jump slightly at the sound of someone's voice next to me. I look up and to my left and see Tristan.

"I'm sorry. I didn't mean to startle you," he says,

"It's okay," I say and stand to give him a hug.

I sit down again and Tristan takes a seat on the arm of the loveseat.

"Zara said she was going to get you to come out tonight, but I wasn't sure if she'd be able to convince you," Tristan says.

Tristan and Zara go out together quite frequently while I usually opt to stay in. They met in high school, both going to an ultra exclusive private school. Zara's parents had certain expectations and ideals for what her life would look like, including her schooling. She hated the school but she and Tristan became good friends while she was there. They were thick as thieves, so much so that they almost got expelled together for underage drinking in the dorms. But someone's father paid a hefty donation and everything was swept under the rug.

"She almost didn't," I reply with a laugh. "But I'm glad I came. The place is really nice."

"Thank you. It turned out well so I can't complain."

Zara appears with two martini glasses and hands one of them off to me before she sits down. I take a sip, my taste buds hit first with the sweetness of the mixer and then the sting of the liquor.

"I wasn't expecting to see you down here," Zara says to Tristan.

"I just came down to check in with everything."

"Don't you have people for that?" Zara asks.

"I do, but I like to be hands on at first, make sure I know the ins and outs of what's going on before I step away."

Tristan stands and holds his hand out to me. "Come on, no reason for y'all to be down here. I have a spot for you upstairs."

7
Sonny

THE OPENING IS GOING better than I ever expected. The turn out for the soft opening has been amazing and I'm proud of the success that Oasis is already having. I hoped it would be successful, to my core I knew it would be, but still as the day approached doubt began to seep in and I couldn't shake the fear that this soft opening would be unsuccessful. A flop. A tangible representation of my failure. But it isn't. My name isn't publicly attached to Oasis, though it's not a secret that I have been involved but I wanted Oasis to exist on its own and not just in conjunction with me or my popularity.

This soft opening was fueled only by word of mouth, both Tristan and I invited people to come and gave those people the ability to invite people they knew too. We used this smaller opening as a test to see how things would go and see any areas where we needed to change or improve. I rest my hand on the balcony overlooking the first floor, the other holds my drink, something from Oasis's specials menu that I can't remember the name of.

The DJ transitions into a classic hype song and the crowd goes crazy, the energy in the building electric. Behind me my friends are taking another round of shots. Some of them are from Chicago, some that flew out from LA, but for the most part everyone is getting along which is no small feat when you bring different friend groups together. I slipped away from the group to take in this moment alone, to just soak in this success that is so foreign from what I'm used to. Foreign altogether, these past few years.

A hand slips around my bicep and a warm body presses into me. Essence looks up at me. Essence entered the music scene a few years ago, right around the time when I didn't resign my contract with the label. She dropped hit after hit and quickly gained success. I wouldn't say that we're friends but the industry is small, we're in the same circle.

"What's got you over here all by yourself?" Essence asks.

Her close proximity to me allows me to hear her over my friends singing and rapping along to the song in our section.

"Just taking a minute to take it all in."

"It's a pretty great space. You did a good job."

"Thank you," I say. "I had a lot of help though so I can't take all the credit."

"You've been a hard man to get a hold of, lately."

"What do you mean?" I ask.

"My manager has been trying to contact yours but he's been getting the run around. And then you up and left LA, so its not like you've been around."

"What is this about?"

"I think we'd be good together," she says, her voice low and suggestive. "On a song I mean."

I don't miss the double meaning in her statement. The sultry gaze she gives me while still wrapped against my arm makes it apparent but I don't engage. I don't want a fling right now, the lack of emotional attachment hasn't been appealing to me for a while now. Not saying that I haven't engaged in them when that itch is too much for me and my hand to solve on my own. But one woman has been on my mind since I ran into her again after years and that woman isn't Essence.

"I'm not releasing music right now Essence. You know that."

"I know," she replies, shifting closer into me. "But I just thought you might change your mind if I asked you myself."

Over her head I see three figures coming up the stairs, Tristan first and then two women behind him. I saw Tristan earlier in the night and can tell it's him but the women's faces are shadowed from the low light and distance. They don't walk in my direction, the opposite actually as Tristan leads them towards the booth that he reserved for himself. The woman in the back turns her head to the side, looking around upstairs, and recognition hits.

"Sonny?" Essence says, trying to get my attention.

"What?" I ask, taking my eyes off Laila to look at her.

"I said that I have a song that I would love for you to be on. But your manager keeps shutting mine down without even sending you the demo."

I slide my arm out of Essence's grasp and step back away from her.

"I appreciate it Essence, but the answer is still no. Excuse me."

I step away from the railing and Essence, wholly uninterested in whatever she was trying to say to me.

On three separate occasions Laila and I have run into each other without any planning from either of us. I'm not usually a guy that subscribes to the idea of fate or something being meant to be, but I also don't believe that these situations are all just by happenstance anymore either.

One time is chance.

Two times is coincidence.

Three times is …

I'm not sure of the last word for that saying but unintentionally running into Laila is something that I don't want to just let pass. So I follow this unexplainable pull that I have to this woman and make my way over to where she sits in the booth with Tristan and her friend that I now see is the same friend that I saw on her Instagram.

I slide into the booth next to Tristan, setting my glass down on the table.

"What are you doing here?" Laila says, a scowl on her face when she sees that it's me.

"I could ask you the same thing," I reply, locking eyes with her. We hold each other's gaze for a long moment. I want to reach out and smooth her scrunched eyebrows but I don't, instead I take a sip from my glass before setting it back down on the table.

I break eye contact and turn to Tristan. "It seems like everything is going well."

"I told you it would, there was no doubt about it," he replies.

"That's not an answer," Laila interrupts.

I turn my focus back to Laila and take her in. Her hair is loose in natural curls flowing over her shoulders and down her back and at this moment I decide that it's my favorite way that she's worn her hair that I've seen so far. Her dark brown eyes glare at me waiting for a response, some sort of explanation for why I've invited myself to their table.

"Tristan and I opened Oasis together," I finally reply. "A joint venture if you will. And I thought I'd come say hello."

"You two know each other?" Tristan asks.

"Something like that," I reply, my gaze focused on Laila. "Somehow we keep running into each other."

"Keep?" her friend questions.

"Yeah, keep," I reply holding my hand out to her. "I'm Sonny by the way."

She takes my hand and gives it a soft shake. "Zara."

"I ran into Bryce when I went to that bar downtown a few weeks ago," Laila says pointedly towards Zara.

Zara's eyes go wide. "Wait is that when you were -"

"Yep." Laila cuts her off.

Bryce.

I like the way my name sounds coming from her lips. There are very few people in my life who call me Bryce and that number of people goes down drastically if you subtract my family from the picture. It's not often that I introduce myself because people usually already know who I am, but even when I do I use 'Sonny' and not 'Bryce'. But with Laila all those years ago I offered my government name freely.

Tristan reaches into the inside pocket of his suit jacket and pulls out his phone, checking the name of the caller.

"Excuse me I have to take this," Tristan says, bringing the phone to his ear and standing from the booth.

As Tristan leaves, one of the VIP servers stops at our booth and asks if she can get us anything. I decline, happy with the half full drink that I still have but Zara and Laila order another round for themselves.

"Soooo Sonny, or is it Bryce," Zara says with a mischievous grin in Laila's direction.

"Sonny is fine," I reply smiling, catching on to the emphasis that Zara is putting on to the fact that Laila calls me Bryce.

"Right, Sonny, I didn't realize you and my dear friend knew each other so well," Zara says.

"I wouldn't say that we know each other well. Maybe just the beginning. But your friend here tends to be busy and isn't the best at returning texts so I thought I would come over and say hello."

"Oh really," Zara replies, intrigued.

Our server stops by our table, dropping off the drinks they ordered and then disappearing again.

"Yeah but I guess I should have anticipated that. She didn't really want to take my number in the first place."

"She is stubborn as hell."

"I can tell," I say, chuckling.

"Y'all do know I'm sitting right here, right?" Laila says, looking between Zara and me.

"Yes, but you like to keep all the juicy details to yourself."

"Juicy details?! There is nothing juicy to tell," Laila argues.

"You're sitting here calling this man by his government name and you wanna say there's nothing to tell?! Girl please."

I chuckle because her friend does have a point.

Zara turns to me and props her elbows on the table and folds her hands. "So how long has this thing been going on between the two of you."

"A little while," I reply with a shrug.

"Well I guess I'll give you two some time to catch up then."

Zara turns and whispers something in Laila's ear and then Laila whispers something back. Zara stands from the table and picks up her drink. She doesn't say anything to me but the fierce look she sends in my direction expresses her message loud and clear.

Don't fuck with my friend.

"Continuing to stalk me?" I say with a smirk.

"Stalk you!?!" Laila asks incredulously. "I didn't even know you were going to be here. And you're the one who came over here."

"Touché. Why didn't you tell me you were coming here tonight?"

"It wasn't my idea, Zara wanted to come."

I lean forward, placing my elbows on the table. "Do you believe in fate, Laila?"

She scrunches up her nose at my question. "What?"

"Fate. Destiny. A higher power. God. I don't know, whatever you want to call it."

Laila looks at me confused with where I'm going with my line of questioning so I continue.

"I wouldn't consider myself religious. A believer maybe, but my family were one of the ones who went to church for Christmas and Easter at most. I don't usually put a lot of weight into the idea of things like fate. But I think my feelings are changing."

"And why is that?"

"You."

"Me?"

"Yeah, you," I reply taking a sip of my drink. "This gorgeous ass girl who I keep running into in ways that shouldn't happen. Hell, until a few weeks ago I didn't even live here. Yet on three separate occasions we've crossed paths. Unintentionally on both of our parts. And I just can't accept that it means nothing."

Laila's gaze is focused on the table in front of her as she plays with one of her curls, stretching it and then letting it bounce back into itself. "It doesn't have to mean anything. Coincidences happen all the time."

"They do, but I think this is different."

"Of course you do," Laila says.

"What does that mean?"

Laila finally looks up and locks eyes with me. "I'm sure this whole 'you're different' talk works often for you, but I'm not interested so you don't have to waste your time."

Her words bring a grin of amusement to my face. She thought I was running game. Just trying to say anything to get some pussy. But I honestly wasn't. Laila intrigued me and I wanted to explore that. Would I fuck her if that's what she wanted, absolutely, but I wanted more than that.

"Whoever let you believe that any time spent with you is being wasted, deserves his ass kicked," I reply simply.

"Something we agree on," Laila says. "But I'm still not interested in being one of the many women you have in cities all around the world. I'm also not delusional enough to compete with anyone else."

"There is no competition."

"I find that hard to believe."

"There is no competition," I repeat. "Do I enjoy the company of a woman from time to time? I'm single, so of course. But when

I'm in a relationship and someone is mine, they get all of me, no sharing. I would never disrespect a woman by cheating on her."

Laila stares in my eyes trying to gauge whether I'm telling the truth or not. I hold her gaze, showing her the sincerity of my words until she breaks eye contact and looks away.

"Let's make a deal," I say, grabbing her attention again.

"I'm not looking for anything from you, Bryce."

"You haven't even heard what I'm offering," I say, finishing off my drink.

"What are you offering?"

"Friendship. Let's be friends."

Laila scowls at me, most likely in disbelief that my intentions are actually to just get to know her.

"No."

She says it with finality in her tone and the brutal honesty of it takes me by surprise. Of any outcome I would have come to, Laila turning me down was not one I expected. Though I guess that is a mistake on my part seeing as Laila has been nothing but direct and honest from the very first moment I met her. In fact it's been one of the things that has drawn me most to her, along with the fact that she's fucking beautiful.

"Why not?"

The shock must be evident on my face.

"You really aren't used to people turning you down huh?" she says, sitting back with a smug look on her face.

"One, I find it hard to believe that you have very many platonic friends who are women," she continues.

I open my mouth to argue that point but I come up empty. "Alright you might be right. But that doesn't mean I can't start now."

"Two, if we become friends that means I become a part of your orbit. I'll be on the radar in connection with you and I don't want that. I don't want people following me around all in my business. I just want to live my life.

Before I can respond I hear my name called out from the other side of the room.

"SONNY! Bring your ass over here!" One of my friends calls out from the group of tables that I abandoned to come to Laila's booth. I look over to my friends and see one of them with his arms up, trying to get my attention. Shots are being passed out and by the smiles on everyone's faces, they're having a good time.

"Go," Laila says as someone yells out for me again.

"Join me."

"Nah, not my vibe," she says, shaking her head.

I nod and stand. I grab her hand, feeling the softness and warmth of her fingers in mine, trying my best to commit the feeling to memory. I desperately want to bring Laila along with me, to extend the time of her being here with me but I also respect her too much to try to force her to do something she doesn't want to do.

"I hear you, but it doesn't have to be like that. You won't have to be in the spotlight at all. Just think about it," I say, squeezing her hand softly before I let it go.

8
Laila

MY HEAD IS POUNDING. I crack my eyes open and the onslaught of the bright sun streaming through my curtains makes the thumping in my head more intense. The room is spinning slightly but just enough to make me nauseous. I send a quick thanks to past Laila who had the forethought to leave Advil and a glass of water on my nightstand. I pick the Advil up and pop two of the pills into my mouth and drink all of the water.

I groan and force myself out of bed and to my bathroom to do my morning routine. Shower. Teeth brushed. Skin care. Moisturize. I feel slightly better after all of that but my head is still pounding. I open the door to my bedroom and walk out to the living room and kitchen. Zara is in the kitchen, humming to herself.

"Morning."

"Good morning," Zara says with a smile that drops as soon as she turns around and sees me. "Oh boo, you look rough."

I glare at her as I sit in one of the stools at the kitchen island. "You're chipper this morning."

"Good dick will do that to you," she replies, a mischievous look in her eyes. "Which I thought you would relate to this morning buuut.."

After Bryce left to hang out with his friends I went back downstairs to find Zara. One of her guys, Aaron I think, or maybe Ashton? Shit, I can't remember the man's name. We danced and drank but eventually I was ready to go home. Zara offered to leave with me but she was still having a good time so I told her to stay with Ashton/Aaron and I took a rideshare home by myself.

"Oh shut up," I say laughing. "I didn't sleep with Bryce."

"Wait a minute." Zara turns to face me with an accusing finger pointed at me. "Don't think you're getting out of talking about him. Why didn't you tell me you had run into him again?"

"I don't know, I guess I just didn't want to make it a big deal."

"It is a big deal though."

I groan and lay my head on my arm on the counter. "You sound like him."

"Well then both of us are right because that doesn't just 'happen'."

"People run into each other all the time. It's nothing special."

"So running into a fine ass celebrity multiple times has happened to you before."

"Well no, but -"

"Exactly!" she says, cutting me off. "You're acting all nonchalant like its normal shit for you."

"It doesn't matter what it is because I'm not interested in making it anything and neither is he."

"His fine ass is definitely interested in you."

"Shut up, no he's not."

"Friend, I saw the way he was staring you down across that table. I'm not tryna hear any of that. He looked like he would've taken you right then and there on that table if you said you were down."

"Zara!" I exclaim.

"What?" she says, shrugging. "I'm just telling you what I saw."

"No matter what you *saw* it's not happening. He said he just wants to be friends."

"So if he just wants to be friends and that's what you want too, why is your face all scrunched up."

I relax my face, now acutely aware of the frown I was making. "This is why I didn't want to talk to you about him."

"You didn't want me to call you out on your bullshit. I get that. But as your best friend it's kinda a part of my job description."

My phone dings with notifications and I grab my phone to check them.

"I bet you that's him right there."

I'm glad that I didn't take her up on that bet because there it is right at the top of my notifications, a text from Bryce. My face must give it away because Zara does a little shoulder shimmy and says in a singsong voice, "I told you."

sonny

I want to see you again. What are you doing today?

Friend.

"He wants to see me again," I say, chewing on my bottom lip.

"Why do you look so upset about that?"

"I'm not upset, I'm just..."

I let my sentence trail off because I have no idea what I feel. Anxious? Nervous? Confused? Shit, all of the above? I take a deep breath and lock my phone, leaving him on read.

"I'm not upset because I'm not going to see him again," I say.

"Why not?" Zara asks, confused.

"Because I," I pause, grasping for a reason, any reason. "Just because!"

"Oh shit, you like him," Zara says in a singsong voice.

"I do not! I don't even know him."

"Then give me one good reason why you don't want to see him again. You've apparently been texting him for weeks. And 'just because' is not a good reason."

"If you really don't want to go then don't, you know I will always support your decisions," Zara says. "But I think you're just scared of whatever this 'thing' is between you two. And you shouldn't let that stop you."

I let out a deep sigh, making up my mind and pick up my phone. I type a quick text.

me

What did you have in mind?

sonny

I was thinking brunch

***

I am still unsure about being friends with Bryce but even with all my reservations, I wanted to see him again too. So I agree to brunch because 'if a nigga wants to wine and dine you, who are you to stop him?'. Zara's words, not mine but she's not wrong.

Bryce sends me the address and I look it up when I see it's a place I've never been to before in downtown Rosewood. The weather has warmed up enough that all of the snow has melted so my train ride and walk to the restaurant isn't bad.

He told me that it would be private and that I didn't have to worry about anything, but my guard is still up when I reach the restaurant. I open the door and step in, expecting the loud hustle and bustle of other people eating and being served but I'm met with just the soft background music of the restaurant. The dining room is completely empty. Off to my right a couple of employees are talking and laughing while they roll silverware in napkins. One of them notices me and steps away from the group towards me.

"Laila?"

"Um, yeah," I reply. "I was supposed to meet someone here, but I must have got the address wrong."

"Nope you're in the right place, follow me," he says.

He leads me to the back of the restaurant to a secluded area. When we step through the glass doors, my breath catches. The room has windows on three of the walls and the roof, allowing tons of natural light to filter in. Plants and greenery are all over the room, in planters, hanging from the ceiling, climbing up the trellises against the walls. It's magical. I'm sure the space is usually filled with multiple tables but today there's only one, right in the middle and sitting in one of the chairs is Bryce with a big smile on his face.

The hostess leads me to the table before he leaves, telling us that our server will be with us in a minute. Bryce stands and walks around to my side of the table to pull out my chair for me and the act catches me off guard. A guy has never done that for me before. I unzip my coat and slide my arms out, hanging it on the back of my chair.

Bryce takes his own seat and just looks at me, his eyes locking intently with mine. My face heats and I try hard to stop the physical reaction I feel from Bryce's eyes on me, but my body decides not to listen.

"So, what do you think?" Bryce asks.

I take another look around, admiring the beauty of the room before I respond.

"It's really pretty. I know you said it would be private, but I wasn't expecting you to empty out the entire restaurant."

"You stated your conditions. And I wanted to see you again so I found a way to make it happen."

I check my nonexistent watch. "It's been like 12 hours."

"My point still stands."

I jokingly roll my eyes at him and he chuckles. Our waitress comes up to our table, setting down two glasses of water for us and handing us each a menu as well as a specials menu.

"Hi, I'm Charlotte, I'll be taking care of you. Would you like anything else to drink? We have coffee, tea, fresh squeezed juice and mimosas."

My stomach churns at the mention of more alcohol, my body barely recovered from last night's drinking.

"Can I have some orange juice, please," I say.

Charlotte nods and turns to Bryce for his response.

"I'll have some orange juice as well and coffee, black."

"Great, I'll go grab those and give you some time to look over the menu."

We quietly look over our menus and place our order when Charlotte comes back with our drinks.

Bryce picks up his mug and I can't help it when my face scrunches at the large sip of coffee he takes.

"What? You don't like coffee?"

"No I do, I just like my coffee to not taste like coffee."

"Oh so you want milk and sugar with a dash of coffee," he says.

"Precisely, why would I ever want to drink that bitter bean juice straight."

Bryce shakes his head, amused, and sets his mug down on the table.

Without the menu to occupy my hands I don't know what to do with them, so I just fidget with them in my lap. We sit in quiet, not talking and not looking at each other until Bryce clears his throat and I look up meeting his gaze and when our eyes lock, we both burst out laughing. I laugh hard, at just how awkward things have started out, covering my face with my hands until the laughter subsides.

"Soooo," Bryce says. "This is awkward huh."

"You could say that."

"I did all the work to get you here and then ain't got shit to say."

I giggle again. "Why don't you tell me about you? We talked about me when we ran into each other but not about you."

Bryce takes another sip of his coffee. "There's not much to tell. I finished my tour and decided not to resign with my label. Well I guess I knew before it ended that I didn't want to sign. So I've just been on my own taking a break and then realized there wasn't anything keeping me in LA anymore, so I moved back home to Chicago."

Our waitress, Charlotte, comes back to our table with our food, setting our plates down in front of us. She asks if there's anything else she can get for us before leaving again. We pause our conversation to take our first bites of food. I do a small happy dance when I take my first bite because the food is delicious and I was hungrier than I thought.

"Does that little dance mean I did a good job picking the restaurant?"

I hadn't realized he was watching me.

"Nah don't get bashful now," Bryce says.

"That seems like a whole lot of change for you," I say, changing the subject back to what we were talking about before.

He shoots me a look that tells me he knows what I'm doing, but he goes along with me anyway.

"In some ways it has been, but everything has just felt right. Making music will always have my heart, but I lost myself for a while."

I nod in understanding. "I get that."

"What about you? If that awkward silence told us anything, we really don't know each other," Bryce says. "You work for a beauty company right?"

"Yeah, I've worked there since my senior year in college. It was just an internship then, but the owner and I became really good friends so I accepted the job when she offered it after I graduated."

"It sounds like you really like it."

"Yeah I do," I reply. "My job has kind of become my life lately, but I really enjoy the work that I do so I don't mind."

My phone rings, interrupting our conversation. I grab it from my purse but quickly decline the call when I see that it's my mom.

"You can take that if you need to," Bryce says.

"No it's just my mom."

I'm cut off by my phone ringing again. I sigh heavily and send my mom to voicemail again, certain that it isn't anything I can't deal with later. This time I put my phone on 'do not disturb' before I drop it into my bag. Anyone important will still be able to reach me, but she is not one of those people.

"I take it you guys aren't close."

I scoff. "You could say that. She usually only calls when she needs something from me."

"Damn, I'm sorry."

"Don't be. It is what it is," I reply nonchalantly. "Are you close with your family?"

"For sure. My sisters are a lot older than me so sometimes it felt like I had three moms growing up but we all get along well."

"What's the age gap?"

"Lauryn is twelve years older than me and Shannon is thirteen years older," Bryce says.

"Oh you're really the baby *and* the only boy," I say. "I bet you were spoiled rotten."

"Shit, if you let my sisters tell it, hell yeah," he says laughing. "According to them I could get away with murder and my parents wouldn't have batted an eye."

I giggle at his exaggeration. "So are you denying it?"

Bryce gives a devious grin. "I was an angel child and I deny all allegations otherwise."

"That tells me all I need to know!" I say.

"Are you speaking from experience or are you just being a youngest child hater?"

"Hater? I would never," I say, taking mock offense. "I grew up as an only child, but I have younger siblings on my dad's side."

"You firing shots at me is crazy considering you've probably never had to share anything in your entire life."

"Oh whatever," I reply laughing. "My sharing skills are just fine, thank you very much."

Bryce grins, the dimples in his cheeks appearing.

Charlotte returns to clear away our empty dishes. She asks us if we need anything else but we both shake our heads no and she leaves again.

"Are you close with them?" Bryce asks.

"Hmm?" I ask, not sure what he's referring to.

"Your dad and siblings."

"Oh. Umm not really. My parents weren't ever technically together and my dad moved to Texas when I was young so I never saw him that often. He got married a while ago and he and his wife had twins."

"I'm sorry to hear that."

I haven't thought about my dad and his family in a while. Some sadness tries to creep up but I shrug it off, firmly pushing the emotions away.

"It's really not that big of a deal."

"So, *friend*," Bryce says, shifting the conversation. "What do you have planned for the rest of the day?"

"Honestly, I don't have much planned. I have some things for work to do, but nothing exciting."

"Work on a Saturday, your job really is your life. We can't have that," Bryce says, tossing his napkin onto the table. "How about we go on an adventure instead."

"Adventure?" I ask, confused. "What would we do on this adventure?"

"I would tell you but that would spoil all the fun."

I chew on my bottom lip, unsure if I want to accept his offer or not. Bryce looks at me, waiting for a response and the hopeful look in his eyes sends flutters to my belly.

"I guess our adventure awaits."

9
Laila

"Did you drive here?"

"No, I took the train," I reply.

"Bet, you can ride with me then. My car is parked right down the street." Bryce says.

We both stand and walk back through the restaurant to the front entrance. He thanks the staff for taking care of us and his words are so sincere. Bryce takes a beanie and sunglasses from the pocket of his coat and puts them on before he holds the door to the restaurant open for me.

He really is trying to fight those asshole allegations, damn.

"Since when did you start being nice?" I ask.

"I've been trying to tell you all along that I am nice."

"The jury is definitely still out on that one."

The walk to the parking garage where Bryce's car is parked is short. He hands his ticket to the valet attendant and they leave to get the car for us.

"I'm surprised you drive yourself around," I say. "Don't celebrities usually have drivers or something?"

"A lot of people do, but that's never been my thing. When Xavier and I are together, he drives us a lot but other than that I usually drive myself around."

A Lamborghini Urus pulls up and stops in front of us. It's blacked out with dark tint all around. The valet attendant steps out and hands the key to Bryce. Bryce takes the key and comes to the passenger side of the car and opens my door. I thank him and get into the car and he shuts the door before rounding the car and getting in himself.

Bryce drives out of the parking garage and merges into the flow of traffic. The sun shines down brightly, a significant contrast to the usual overcast, gloomy weather that is typical for the end of January. Downtown Rosewood is alive with people shopping, running errands and simply enjoying the sunshine.

"How do you manage going out without running into fans all the time?" I ask curiously.

"It's not as hard as you think," Bryce says looking over at me.

"So you just casually walk around Target buying toothpaste and toilet paper? I find that hard to believe."

"Well, no," he says with a smile. "I usually get those things delivered, but I could if I wanted to. Especially in Los Angeles, people are used to seeing celebrities all of the time so it isn't a big deal. And if you don't go to known places where paparazzi hang out or call them yourself you can usually fly under the radar. People and their cell phones are a whole different thing though."

"How do you get around that?"

Bryce shrugs. "Sometimes you can't. If X is around and he sees people trying to take a picture or video he'll tell them not to. But usually, if I'm going out and I really don't want to be noticed I wear hats," he says, pointing to the beanie on his head. "And sunglasses."

I nod in understanding.

"You sort of get used to it, though. And there's a ton of people that you don't see unless they want you to," Bryce says.

"I'll have to take your word for it," I reply.

"I heard you when you said that you don't want to be in my 'orbit'. I'm going to do everything I can to honor that, okay?"

Bryce's words feel genuine and I feel a squeezing in my chest at the idea that he's taking my wants so seriously. I decide to focus on other things instead of the warm feelings in my chest that are trying to keep my attention.

"You talked shit about my work being my life, but isn't that true for you too? Touring and releasing albums and all that doesn't just happen. That takes a lot of time and hard work."

"It does, but that doesn't mean I don't have hobbies or take time off. Hell, it's been almost four years since I was on tour."

"What are these hobbies?" I ask skeptically.

"I thought you'd never ask," Bryce says smiling. "We're actually going somewhere for one of my hobbies now."

The drive to this mystery location takes about thirty minutes. Bryce pulls off the main street and goes down a back alley. He parks the car behind what looks like a warehouse with only one other car in the small lot.

"I swear if you're planning on taking me in there to murder me, I will haunt you for the rest of your life."

Bryce throws his head back and laughs. He kills the engine and gets out of the car and walks around to the passenger side and opens my door. He holds his hand out to help me out of the car but I don't take it.

"I am so serious," I deadpan, a serious look on my face.

"Come on. I promise you won't be murdered."

I give him another skeptical glance before I take his hand and slide out of the car. The back door to the warehouse opens and a white woman with long blonde hair and a fitted pantsuit steps out, holding the door open with her back. We get closer and she speaks.

"Mr. Taylor, welcome in."

"Thank you," Bryce replies.

We step into the building and follow the woman down a hallway that is not very well lit. I keep my guard up, really wishing that I had actually kept up with those boxing classes Zara and I took all of two times. The end of the hallway has another door with 'showroom' on it in faded letters that were probably once white. The woman pulls the door open and we step into a large room full of ... pianos? There are over a dozen pianos spread across the room, the bright overhead lights shining against the shiny wood.

I turn around to look at Bryce, frowning.

Bryce grins. "You should've seen the look on your face when we went down that hallway. Your ass was so scared."

I smack him lightly with the back of my hand.

"You're the one who brought me to a back entrance and down a dark dingy hallway. I didn't know what to expect!"

"You never have to be worried about your safety with me, Laila. I won't ever hurt you and I will never let anyone else hurt you when I'm around either."

There it is again. Those little flutters in the base of my belly that spark whenever I'm around Bryce.

"Would you like anything to drink? Sparkling water? Champagne." The woman who escorted us in asks with a tight lipped smile.

Bryce answers for the both of us. "Champagne is fine."

Champagne and pianos... what in the actual fuck is going on.

"I'll be just a moment, but feel free to have a look around the showroom."

She disappears to a back room and then it's only me and Bryce.

"You brought me to a piano showroom?" I ask, still confused.

Bryce walks further into the room, running the pads of his fingers over the lacquer of the top of a black grand piano.

"Yeah I guess I did. Is that weird?"

"I wouldn't say weird," I reply. "But it is a first for me."

"I made this appointment a few weeks ago, before I knew we would go to brunch. I had to leave my old piano back in LA so I came to pick out a new one for my place here."

The blonde woman comes back with two flutes of champagne in her hands, the bubbles still floating to the top of the light gold liquid. She hands each of us a flute before she speaks.

"Please take your time looking around, Mr. Taylor. We do have the one that you inquired about in our special collections room off to your right. Please let me know if you need anything or have any questions."

"Thank you," Bryce says.

"I didn't know you played piano."

Bryce moves on to another piano. To me it looks the same as a handful of other pianos in the room but I'm sure there are specs and details that I, someone who has never even touched a grand piano, has no knowledge of.

"Growing up my parents had one of our neighbors that they were close with, watch me until they got off of work when I was too young to stay home alone. She had this really old upright piano and she taught me how to play and how to read music."

"Aw that's sweet. That was really nice of her," I say.

Bryce shakes his head. "I'm not sure anyone would say Mrs. Roberts was sweet. She was kind of a grumpy old lady. Like the kind who yelled at you for being on her grass."

I snort, the imagery of a young Bryce being scolded by a little old lady sitting on her porch coming to mind.

"I'm sure there was a couch in her house you weren't allowed to sit on too."

"For sure," he replies. "It was floral and covered in plastic and she didn't let anyone sit on it."

We walk through the pianos, sipping our champagne. I stop and run my fingers over the keys of a dark brown piano that's smaller than the other ones in the room.

"What do you think?" Bryce asks.

I shrug my shoulders. "I mean they're clearly really nice, but they all just look like pianos to me."

Bryce nods in understanding. "Some people probably have a really complex way to tell them apart, but for me it's kind of like anything that you have a preference on. Sometimes you have a really strong preference for something and sometimes it's just one of many that a bunch of different companies have made."

"That makes sense, but how do you pick one then?"

"Trial and error. Just sitting and playing with them until there's one that just feels right."

"So which one is the one that feels right for you," I ask.

Bryce gestures towards the room that the woman referred to earlier. "Let me show you."

The pianos in this room are clearly more custom. While the pianos in the main room were all black or brown there are pianos in here with more unique coloring, white, red and green and even some with a contrasting color on the inside of the lid. One piano in particular is separated away from the others on a platform.

Bryce leads us to that piano, it's black with gold accents but instead of being shiny it has a satin finish. Bryce pulls out the piano bench and gestures for me to sit down. I sit and hold my flute in both of my hands, being careful not to spill any champagne on the instrument that I know for sure costs more than my annual salary. Bryce sets his empty champagne flute down on the floor next to the piano leg and sits next to me on the bench. The side of his arm brushes against mine as he positions his fingers on the keys. He closes his eyes and takes in a deep breath, exhaling slowly, and then he begins to play. I don't immediately recognize the song, it's familiar but the name escapes me until he plays a few more notes, getting further into the verse.

Ain't No Sunshine by Bill Withers.

I watch Bryce's hands as he deftly slides across the keys, playing the notes of the song. His movements are fluid and certain and though he isn't singing I can feel the emotion of the song just from the notes he plays. I am so engrossed in watching him play that I don't realize the song is over until the sound of the last note lingering stops, leaving the room in silence.

"Wow that was beautiful," I say..

"Thank you," Bryce says. "That was one of Mrs. Roberts' favorite songs so it was one of the first ones I memorized."

I smile softly at Bryce, those damn flutters in my belly making an appearance once again.

"Why didn't you bring your piano from LA?" I ask, trying to get out of my own head about the feelings I definitely didn't want to be having.

"I left most of my things in my LA house. I'm not planning on selling it right now so it made more sense to me to get something that'll fit the place I'm in right now better."

"So Chicago is just temporary for you then?"

"Chicago will always be home. But I'm not sure if it'll be where I am long term."

"Oh, okay."

Bryce looks at me and tilts his head to the side slightly, his eyes dancing around my face.

"What?" I ask, confused by the way he's looking at me.

He shakes his head softly. "Nothing, you're just hard to read sometimes."

I want to ask him what he means by that but my phone starts to ring. I glance to see who's calling and I see Cass' name on the screen.

"I'm sorry it's work, I have to take this," I say standing from the bench.

I step down from the platform and walk a few feet away, turning my back to Bryce to answer my call.

"Hey Cass, what's up?" I ask when the call connects.

"Hey I know it's Saturday, but I need to ask you a huge favor."

"Is everything okay? What's going on?"

"The delivery dates for the new toners and serums got mixed up so instead of coming on Monday they're being delivered today. I tried to call Reagan but she didn't answer."

Cass' words are rushed and her voice sounds mildly panicked.

"I hate that I even have to ask this of you but we've been waiting so long for this shipment so that we can restock. And you remember the last shipment we weren't there for the delivery for was stolen and I would do it myself but I'm down in Indianapolis with Cyrus-"

"Cass," I say, cutting her off.

"Yeah?"

"I need you to take some deep breaths."

I hear the sounds of her inhale and exhale through the phone, once and then twice and then I speak.

"I will handle the shipment. You don't even have to worry about it. You enjoy your time with Cyrus okay?"

"Are you sure because I can come back tonight to -"

"Yes I'm sure," I reassure her. "I will handle it and I'll see you on Monday. Tell Cyrus I said 'hello'."

"You're a fucking godsend, Laila. Thank you so much."

I end the call and turn around to see Bryce standing near the door to the room, one hand in his pocket as he scrolls on his phone with the other.

"Everything okay?" he asks as I walk towards him.

"I'm sorry I have to go, my boss needs me to handle a shipment that's getting delivered."

"No worries, I can take you wherever you need to go."

"Are you sure? You probably have more important things to do anyway. I don't want to get in the way with that."

Bryce shakes his head. "Laila you can't get in the way when there isn't anything there. Think of this as another part of the adventure. I showed you a piece of my world and now I want to see a piece of yours."

***

I unlock the delivery door and walk in, letting the door close behind me.

"It's nothing special," I say, trying to keep expectations low. "It's just our warehouse and office space."

I'm flipping on the lights in the office when I hear the ring of the doorbell announcing the arrival of the delivery. I walk back to the door and open it to the delivery driver.

"Can you sign here?" The man asks, holding the signature pad out to me.

I quickly scribble out an illegible squiggle and pass it back to the man. Bryce stands next to me with his sunglasses and beanie on. I wait for the delivery driver to recognize Bryce and say something but he doesn't. He just tucks the signature pad in his pocket and goes to get his dolly to start unloading the boxes.

"Which one is your favorite?" Bryce asks.

He's standing in front of the clear wall mounted shelves that display every product Lovely Day has ever sold. From the very first ones that Cassandra was selling out of her apartment to our last most recent release this past holiday season.

"It used to be this one," I say pointing to our watermelon lip balm.

It's been a part of the mainline for years and I have one with me at all times.

"But my new favorite is actually one from the new collection."

"Really? Which one?"

I walk over to my desk and grab one of the samples of the collection that I kept for myself. I unscrew the lid and take a sniff of the familiar sweet scent.

I walk back over to Bryce and hold it up to Bryce for him to smell too. "This is our vanilla and lemon body butter."

He inhales deeply, closing his eyes and taking in the scent. When he opens his eyes they lock with mine, his gaze so intense that I feel a chill over my body even though I'm still wearing my coat.

He smiles. "I can see why you like it, it's really nice."

I take a step back and screw the top back on to the body butter. "Thank you, you can keep this one if you want."

"I'd like that."

I clear my throat, trying to get rid of the dry feeling that has suddenly appeared. "I'm just going to count the boxes and then make sure everything is here and then we can go."

"Take your time, I'll be here."

10
Sonny

How long does it take to get used to the noises a home makes? The creaks of the floorboards, the sounds of the wind rustling through the trees outside the windows, and the hum of the furnace turning on. The little noises that when you're lying awake at night make it that much harder to fall asleep. How long does it take?

Clearly more than a couple weeks.

It's late and I have to be up early in the morning so I should be knocked out already, but here I am laying in my bed, wide awake staring at the ceiling in the dark because my mind refuses to settle and allow me to sleep. I let out a frustrated groan and toss the covers back to stand from the bed. I slide my bare feet into the slides I leave by my bed and walk to the kitchen. There's enough moonlight shining in from the windows that I don't bother turning on any lights as I go. I yank open the fridge and examine the contents, even though it's fully stocked I don't really want anything from it. I let out another deep sigh as I grab a bottle of water from one of the shelves and close it back.

Instead of going back to my room to fail at my attempts to fall asleep, I go to the living room and take a seat at my piano. Laila made fun of me for caring more about choosing a piano than anything else in my home here, but I already knew I was going to hire an interior designer to figure out all of the other things to make the space look pretty and put together and they did a great job. A piano isn't a necessity for most, but on nights like these I'm happy that I went out of my way to prioritize it.

My lyric journal rests open on the music shelf of my piano where I left it from the last time I sat here, the page filled with scribbled out words from the song I have been trying to piece together for weeks now. I have written hundreds of songs in my life, all of them haven't been good, hell most of them will never even see the light of day. But others I am able to contribute to my success as an artist, or have been picked up by other artists to record and release for themselves. In general songwriting is something that has always come easy to me. Usually it only takes a few days from when I get that spark of inspiration for a song to get to a place where I'm happy with it. But not this one. For some reason every direction I try to take this song in just doesn't feel right yet it's still stuck in my head. I have listened to a bunch of beats to try to spark inspiration, but nothing has helped the lyrics flow.

I set my phone on the music shelf next to the lyric journal and run my fingers over the keys of the piano. I play a few notes and then fall into a made up melody, without any rhyme or reason or particular end goal, just playing whatever feels right. As time passes

I try to work on the song that's been stuck in my head, but I hate every direction I try and end up in the same place that I started.

My phone buzzes and the screen illuminates with the notification.

laila

> I had a long day, I've been trying to put the finishing touches on this collection.

A second later another text comes in.

laila

> Sorry for the late reply, I'm a terrible texter.

Since that first message I sent to Laila, we have consistently kept up a conversation. This afternoon I had asked her how her day was going, but she hadn't replied until now. I pick up my phone, unlocking it and opening the message. I start to type out a response but then change my mind, deleting the words I previously typed and instead initiating a FaceTime. It's a risky decision to start an unprompted FaceTime especially at this time of night and with someone that you don't know super well, but I silently pray it works in my favor.

The call rings for a while and I am sure that it's going to go unanswered until at the last moment the call connects. The camera is pointed towards the ceiling of a dimly lit room.

"You know it's rude to FaceTime someone out of nowhere," Laila says from somewhere off the screen.

"My bad," I apologize. "You said you were a bad texter, so I thought this would be easier for you."

Laila picks up the phone and her face comes on to the screen. Her hair is wrapped in a bonnet and her face is bare, but she's no less beautiful than any other time that I've seen her.

"I guess that's fair," Laila says, her tone softer than before. "I wasn't expecting you to be up."

I run a hand over my hair. "I had some trouble sleeping so I was playing around on the piano for a bit."

"Working on something in particular?"

"Trying to," I say with a chuckle. "It hasn't been going so well."

"I'm sure it'll come to you," Laila replies. "Maybe it's just not the right time for it."

I nod in understanding, knowing that she's probably right, even though it's not the answer that I want to hear.

"You weren't up late working this whole time were you?" I ask knowing that she was probably doing just that.

In the small time that I've known Laila, she's expressed just how important her career is to her and she works hard at it because of it.

"No, I was watching TV and then I remembered I needed to fix something on the website before it goes live. I was doing that when I remembered I never responded to your message."

"Left a nigga on delivered all day," I say joking.

Laila rolls her eyes, but a small smile peaks out of her annoyance.

"In all seriousness, I can tell how much you care about the brand, I just hope you're taking care of yourself as well," I say.

"It's our first launch of the year and it's also the biggest one we've ever done, so I want to make sure it's perfect. But now that's done and I'm watching tv."

I stand from the piano, knowing that I'm not going to get any further with the song and walk back towards my bedroom. "I didn't mean to bother you, I don't want to get in the way of your show."

In my room I turn on the lamp on my bedside table and climb back into my bed, sitting with my back against the headboard.

"It's not a bother," Laila says. "I've seen this show a bunch of times, this is the state championship episode."

"Wait, why are you watching it if you've already seen it before?" I ask.

"It's comforting, I like knowing what's going to happen. And I already know I like the show so I don't have to watch a bunch of episodes just for the writers to ruin it in the last season."

Laila flips the screen on her phone so I can see the episode she's watching. She starts telling me about each of the characters and the premise of the show until eventually we're just watching the episode together.

***

"Mannn look who finally brought his ass back to town."

I look around for the man behind the voice until my eyes land on my friend Chris across the gym. He has a big goofy grin on his face as I walk over to him and the other guys sitting on the bleachers in the gym. When I get close Chris and I dap each other up in greeting.

"Only your loud mouth ass would have this much energy at 5 in the morning," I joke back at Chris.

"Nigga it's good to see you, I thought Chris was lying when he said you were gonna join in on the game," Malik says as I dap him up too.

Chris has had his unserious, class clown personality since we were kids growing up together. His family lived down the street from mine when we were in middle school so we often spent a lot of time at each other's houses. Malik joined our friend group in high school and we have stayed friends ever since, staying connected mainly through social media when I was in LA. Malik and Chris were two of the few people I personally invited to the Oasis soft launch and it had been a good time hanging out with them again. When Chris invited me to join in on their weekly basketball sessions with some other guys they knew, I gladly accepted.

Chris introduces me to the other guys in the gym and I acknowledge them all. I set my duffel bag down on one of the bleachers on the sideline and take out my sneakers to replace the slides I wore into the gym.

"Deuce is sick," Chris says. "So Sonny can take his spot on your team Malik."

"Let's get it," I say.

I finish tying my shoes and stand from the bleachers to join some of the guys already on the court warming up.

***

"That's game," Chris says after one of his teammates makes a layup.

After two games the score is split 1-1. We all walk over towards our bags to get some water and take a small break.

I haven't played a full game of basketball in years, so this break is much needed. I take a long swig of water from my water bottle and take a seat on the bleachers to catch my breath.

Malik looks down at his watch checking the time and then grabs his bag, tossing it over his shoulder.

"Aight I gotta head out," Malik says.

"Tapping out early cause you know your team won't win that next one," Chris says.

"Nah, I gotta get home before baby girl wakes up. I want Jess to be able to sleep in."

"Damn, Malik is in full on dad mode," I joke. "I never thought I'd see the day."

Malik pulls out his phone and shows me the picture on his lock screen. A chunky, smiling baby with warm mahogany skin and only her two front teeth.

"She's beautiful."

"Man, it's true what they say about finding your person. Baby girl and her mom are my whole world."

When we were younger, Malik was the guy who never stayed in a relationship for long and had no interest in settling down, and now he has a fiancée and a beautiful daughter.

Growing up, I saw firsthand what love looked like through my parents' relationship. They loved each other deeply and it made me want that for myself but I haven't found it just yet.

My mind goes to Laila, something I've found myself doing a lot lately. I stayed up way too late talking on the phone with her last night, and I should regret it based on how tired I am now. But

I don't. I enjoyed the simplicity of talking with her and hearing about one of her favorite tv shows.

Chris chest passes me the ball and I catch it, caught off guard and knocked out of my thoughts.

"Let's get this last game going."

11
Laila

I OPT FOR A hand basket instead of a cart in an effort to only buy what I came into the store for, champagne. I resist the temptation to walk down the aisles that have nothing to do with why I am in the store and make my way over to the liquor section. A candle from an end cap that was on the way over did end up in my basket but it's on sale so it practically doesn't count, right? Right.

When I find the aisle I need, I grab two bottles off the shelf and place them in the basket. I contemplate whether that's enough before grabbing another for good measure. I turn to leave the aisle the same way that I came but of course at the end of the aisle a man is standing off to the side looking at bottles of sangria, with his shopping cart blocking the entire aisle, making it impossible to get by.

"Excuse me," I say, trying to get his attention while keeping the annoyance out of my voice.

"Sorry," the man says.

He turns and moves his cart, maneuvering it from the middle of the aisle to off to the side, like it should have been in the first place.

The action gives me a glimpse of his face and I immediately feel sick in the pit of my stomach.

Why does the universe hate me?

I don't know how I didn't recognize him immediately, and I hate that I hadn't, because if I had there is no way that I would have said a damn thing to him. When he sees me recognition hits him as well, but the unease and revulsion that I feel are clearly not reciprocated based on the way he greets me.

"Laila, hey it's good to see you."

The shock from the audacity of those words coming from Devin, as if I am an old friend and not an ex who he manipulated and lied to for years, is immediate. The shock quickly turns into anger and instead of acknowledging him, or his words, I start to walk past him.

"C'mon Laila don't be like that," Devin says in a tone meant to soothe but only makes my blood boil more.

I halt my steps whirling around to face him.

"Don't be like that?" I seethe. "You don't get to tell me what to do or feel after the shit you put me through. Matter fact, don't talk to me at all."

Devin is one of those men who knows he's attractive. His hazel eyes and loose hair texture has given him no shortage of women who have boosted his ego in his life, and unfortunately for over two years I was one of them. The girl on his arm who was 'lucky' to be the one he chose to be with.

Devin and I met at a networking event for small businesses in Rosewood. I had just graduated college and joined *Lovely Day* full time and Cass asked me to go to the event with her. During social hour, Devin approached me and struck up a conversation that led to an exchange in contact information and then later a relationship that lasted for over two years. Things started out great, he was sweet, attentive and charming. He said and did all the right things that made me fall for him, made me fall in love with him. And then somewhere along the way it all changed. He became distant, and secretive, and when I would call him out on it he would tell me it was 'nothing' or 'in my head' so I brushed it off. I believed him until one day he told me that he had a baby on the way with someone else. A real life Confessions Part II.

I couldn't fully see it while I was living it, but once the rose colored glasses were off I saw just how toxic our relationship was. The times where he would invalidate my feelings and cause me to not trust my intuition. The ways he made me feel small in our relationship.

"I know you're probably upset," Devin says. "But there's no need to be dramatic, it was all a misunderstanding-"

At those words I see red and I know that I need to get very far away from him before I catch a charge for laying hands on him in the middle of this store. There are so many things I want to say, including that he's a bitch ass piece of shit and I hope his dick falls off. But I don't say that.

I take a second to calm my rage enough to simply say. "Go to hell, Devin."

This time I don't stop when I turn to walk away, putting as much distance as I can between me and him to buy the contents of my basket and get the fuck out of this store.

***

"Hey," I say when the FaceTime call connects.

"Hey, what's wrong?" Bryce asks.

He's laid out on his couch, relaxed, one arm behind his head and the quiet sounds of his TV in the background.

"What do you mean?" I ask. "I didn't even say two words, I'm fine."

I desperately want that to be true, but even hours after my run in with Devin I feel unsettled. Like he came and infiltrated the safe bubble I've been building for the past eight months that we've been broken up. One run in and all the anger and pain that I thought I was over, came flooding back. I thought that I had tucked that all away when I answered the phone, but clearly not.

"Nah something's bothering you, and that's not nothing. What's going on?"

"What makes you think I'm not fine," I ask with a huff, frustrated that he was able to read me so easily.

"It's not a specific thing. But after all the times we've talked, something is different. Something or someone has dimmed your light, and I don't like that shit."

After I told Bryce that I'm a bad texter, our conversations have shifted to mostly talking on the phone. Nearly everyday we Face-Time and talk about our days, nothing specific or special, just easy, friendly conversation. Sometimes it's only a few minutes other times it's a few hours, but it has become a part of my day that I look forward to

"I just," I pause and take a deep breath. "I just don't want to talk about it right now."

"Aight, that's fair but if you do, I'm here to listen."

I nod, unable to form words because all the anger and irritation I felt has now morphed into appreciation and gratitude of my emotions being seen without having to verbally express them, of someone paying enough attention to notice when things aren't as they usually are. That small act has caused a tightness in my chest and a lump in my throat that doesn't ease until Bryce starts talking again.

"A friend of mine was telling me about a new sushi spot downtown and I thought you might want to go."

My stomach rumbles, reminding me that I have neglected to feed it for most of the day unless you count the iced coffee and croissant that I had hours ago.

"Sushi sounds amazing, but I still don't think being in public together is a great idea."

"Why not?"

"Because I'm not trying to have pictures of me and you together sprawled all over the internet."

"They won't be," Bryce says.

"You can't guarantee that," I argue. "I can see the headlines now 'Singer Sonny seen out with mysterious woman' and then they do a deep dive into my life and find pictures of me from when I was 12 with braces, fully in my awkward stage. No thank you."

"That's not gonna happen," Bryce says. I start to interject but he keeps talking. "And I *can* guarantee that, if you come over instead. I'll get the food delivered and we can watch whatever show that you love so much you can recite it from memory."

I blink hard, shocked by the invitation Bryce just gave. Of all the retorts I expected him to give for my pushback on not wanting to be seen in public, this was not one of them. I chew on my bottom lip contemplating the offer.

"It's not a big deal," Bryce says, picking up on my hesitation. "If you don't want to, that's cool too. I just thought I'd offer."

"That would actually be really nice," I say.

"I'll send you the menu, tell me what you want and I'll place the order."

"Okay," I reply in agreement.

My phone buzzes with a text notification from him and I see two links, one for the restaurant's menu and another for the rideshare he ordered from my place to his.

"Thank you for the ride, you didn't have to do that."

"You don't have to thank me Laila. I asked you to come over, it's the least I could do. I was gonna offer to come get you myself, but I had a feeling you'd shoot a nigga down again."

I giggle at his words.

"Mmhm, like I thought," Bryce says. "When you get here, tell the front desk your name and they'll let you up. Send me what you want and I'll see you soon aight?"

I nod and we end the call. I send him the sushi I want and gather my things to leave my apartment right as the rideshare arrives.

I was expecting Bryce to live in a nice place but the bougie luxury that surrounds me when I walk into the lobby of his building still catches me off guard. The marble floors gleam, as if they have just been polished and are free of any signs of snow or salt that existed right outside the doors.

"Good evening miss," the man at the desk says as I approach. "How can I help you?"

"Hello, I'm here to see someone."

"What's your name?"

"Laila, Laila Eden," I reply.

"Ah yes, welcome Ms. Eden, Mr. Taylor already added you to his approved visitors list just give me one moment."

The man taps away on the computer in front of him for a minute and then hands me a keycard. It's black with the name of the building, *Halcyon*, etched into it with gold lettering. Slightly confused, I look towards the man for guidance, but he simply gestures towards the elevators behind him and says, "Floor 37."

I take the short walk to the elevators and press the call button. The doors almost immediately open and I step on, pressing the '37' button on the keypad. The doors close behind me, but the elevator doesn't move. I start to press the button again but then see why I needed the keycard. I tap it against the nondescript scanner next to the numbers and the elevator is set in motion.

The elevator dings as the doors slide open to the middle of Bryce's living room. I step off of the elevator and take in the large open concept space of the living room, kitchen and dining room all with floor to ceiling windows. The space feels masculine but not like a bachelor pad. Moody with the dark blues, black and gray but not cold.

I hear footsteps from the hallway to my right and then I see Bryce.

"My bad, I meant to be out here when you came up," he says as he crosses the room to me.

He pulls me into a hug, the embrace warm and comforting even though it catches me off guard at first.

He takes my coat and hangs it on a hook by the door and I toe off my boots leaving them there as well.

"The food just got here. Make yourself at home, I'm gonna go grab it."

I opt for a seat on one of the stools at the island in the kitchen and it's only a few minutes before Bryce comes back holding a bag with the food. I playfully snatch the paper bag from Bryce and do a little happy dance as I set it down in front of me on the counter. I rip open the bag, yanking through the staples that held it together, eager to get to the food causing the delicious smells permeating the kitchen.

"You love food a lot for someone who's always forgetting to eat," Bryce says with an amused smile on his face.

"Oh shut up," I reply. "I'm busy and then sometimes I forget, but it's not all the time."

I pull all the containers out of the bag and separate them between us. We both take the lids off the containers and open our chopsticks, pulling them apart with the satisfying 'snap'.

"So you had more than one actual meal today?"

I had breakfast, but I know my iced coffee and croissant lunch won't fly with him so I opt for deflection. "I thought you were trying to cheer me up, not talk shit about my food habits."

"The small smile you just gave let's me know that the shit talking *is* what's cheering you up," Bryce replies.

I glare at him but Bryce gives me a smile in return, one that brings out the dimples in his cheeks and hits me right in the panties.

I look away, busying myself with my sushi to avoid the thoughts in my head that I shouldn't be having about my *friend*. I pick up a piece of my spicy tuna roll, dunk it in soy sauce and pop it into my mouth.

"Anyway," I say after I finish chewing. "How was your day? We didn't really talk about you at all earlier."

"Not bad, was in meetings with my manager, Morgan, damn near all day. She's trying to get me to agree to perform. My boy Dez dropped an album a few months ago, and now he's about to start his tour. He wants me to come out as a special guest for some of his stops on the east coast and perform some of the collabs we did early in my career."

"You don't want to do it?"

"Nah, it's not that really," Bryce says. "Performing is amazing, there's no other experience like it and Dez is cool. He's part of the reason I have the success I have now. He took a chance on a nobody and let me collab on a song and it went crazy. And being on stage with him is always a good time. I guess I always thought that when I performed again it would be for a new project but now it just feels …"

"Like a step back?" I offer when Bryce lets the end of his sentence fall.

"Yeah, I guess so."

"Maybe it is a step back, but that doesn't have to mean the past three years meant nothing. You're not the same person you were then, the previous version of you couldn't have known what you'd want now. It's okay to change your mind."

Bryce picks up his last piece of sushi, putting it in his mouth and chewing before he speaks again. "I know, I just don't know if I want to."

"How long do you have to make your decision?"

"A week. The tour starts next month and I'd need to do some rehearsals."

"Whatever you choose will be the right decision, just follow your gut."

I finish off the last of my food and stand to clear off the counter, taking both of our trash and putting it in the nearby trash can.

"Your friend was onto something with that sushi place, that was really good."

"Yeah I might have to add it to my takeout rotation," Bryce replies.

He walks over to one of his cabinets and takes out a brand new package of oreos and sets them down on the counter next to me.

"C'mon let's go watch your show."

"You bought me Oreos?" I ask, genuinely surprised.

"Isn't that what you're always eating while you watch the show?"

"Yeahhh," I say, drawing out the word.

"Then there's your answer."

Bryce doesn't elaborate, he leaves me in the kitchen and walks over to the living room to sit on the couch and pick up the tv remote.

"What episode do you want to watch," Bryce asks, navigating to the streaming service and selecting the show that I have been most recently binge rewatching.

It doesn't mean anything, it's just cookies. I try to reason with myself.

I follow Bryce to the living room and take a seat on the couch next to him, tucking my feet up under me.

"Let's start from the beginning so you get the full experience."

The show's opening scenes and song plays and I open the pack of oreos, taking one out and happily snacking on it.

"So why don't they like each other?" Bryce asks about the two main characters of the show, halfway through the first episode.

"Because their dad is an asshole," I reply. "He left his girlfriend while she was pregnant and now doesn't recognize their son as his and has brainwashed his other son."

"But he brought his new girl and kid back to the same town where his first kid and his mom lives, and now the brothers go to school together."

"Yep."

Bryce shakes his head. "That's some crazy work."

"That's some of the least crazy things that happen just wait."

My foot falls asleep at the end of the second episode. I move it from the position its been in, stretching it out in hopes that the weird tingling numbness quickly goes away.

"You good?"

"Yeah, it just fell asleep."

"Give it here."

"Hmmm?" I ask confused.

I feel Bryce's hand wrap around my ankle and he pulls my sock clad foot into his lap. He uses his thumb to gently massage the sole of my foot. I relax back into the couch and try to focus back on the episode but I can't focus, not with Bryce moving from the sole of my foot to rubbing the little stretch of exposed skin between where my leggings end and my sock begins. The simple motion that he does seemingly absentmindedly makes my whole body tingle with warmth.

12
Laila

ONE THING ABOUT ME and my friends, we love a good themed event. For Valentine's day each year we always do something together, just us girls to catch up on each other's lives. In past years we've done picnics, paint and sips, movie nights with matching pajamas, and this year we decided on brunch.

"Hey!" Maia says, opening Cass's front door. "It's so good to see you!"

"Thank you, you too," I reply, hugging her and then stepping in the door.

Cass met Maia on the same vacation in Mexico where she and Cyrus reconnected over a year ago. Cyrus was there for his brother's wedding and Maia was the bride. Since then they've become close like sisters and Maia has joined our friend group.

"Cass is still getting ready," Maia says. "I was just finishing setting up some last minute things."

"What's left? I can help."

I set the champagne down on the counter and help Maia with the last minute things to make sure everything is perfectly set up. Cass went all out with the decorations, as we all knew she would.

Everything is pink and red from the utensils and napkins to the balloons floating above our heads on the ceiling. The catered bite size finger foods are laid out in an impressive spread on the kitchen counters with rose petals sprinkled around the serving dishes. As we finish up the front door buzzes and Maia goes over to let in Tiffany, Cass's sister, and shortly after, Reagan and Stella arrive too.

I take pictures of the gorgeous set up on both my phone and polaroid camera for the memories, before we dig into the food and drinks.

A moment later Cass comes out of her bedroom dressed in a pink jumpsuit. She goes around the room giving each of us a hug. She reaches me last, pulling me in for a quick squeeze.

"I'm sorry, what is that?!" Tiffany exclaims when Cass and I pull apart.

We all look to her in shock, wondering what she's referring to but her eyes are locked with Cass who's barely holding back a grin.

"You mean this?" Cass asks, bringing her left hand and the stunning new ring on her ring finger into full view.

I'm not sure how I missed it before, but the marquise cut diamond ring with side clusters on a thin gold band is breathtaking.

"Cassandra!"

We all envelope Cass in more hugs, squealing and talking over each other in happiness.

"Where's the champagne we need to celebrate!" Reagan says.

Reagan pops open one of the bottles of champagne I brought and pours each of us a flute. We raise our glasses in celebration , all of us grinning from ear to ear.

"I can't believe you're engaged!" Maia says. "I'm so happy for you."

"Wedding planning is going to be so fun," Tiffany says. "Have you and Cyrus thought about dates? Or maybe just a season, we can start there."

"So about that," Cass says.

The room goes quiet as we all look over at her wondering what the hell she's talking about.

She takes a big gulp of her champagne and swallows before she replies. "Cyrus and I aren't engaged."

I scrunch my eyebrows in confusion

"What do you mean?" Reagan asks.

"Shut up!" Maia says, catching on before the rest of us. "Where's the champagne we need another toast!"

"We aren't engaged because we got married on Friday," Cass says.

I bring my hand to my mouth, stunned. "What!? No you didn't."

Cass giggles and nods her head. "I did!"

Maia refills our champagne flutes and we raise them again to 'cheers'.

"To my sister," Tiffany says with tears in her eyes. "You're my best friend and I am so happy to get a front row seat to this amazing life you're creating. I love you so much and I'm so happy that you have found your person."

We clink our glasses together and Tiffany and Cass tearfully hug each other. I am overcome with emotion and feel tears well up in my own eyes. I feel so incredibly grateful to be able to share this moment with my friends, in celebration of Cass and Cyrus' union because they truly are meant for each other.

"Okay I know you have pictures. I want to see," Reagan says.

Cass takes out her phone and shows us the beautiful behind the scenes of her and Cyrus getting ready together the day they got married.

"I can't believe you eloped. I literally would have never expected that," I say to Cass, looking at the picture of her in her white dress.

"Honestly me either," she replies. "But on the flight home I just thought why not. I was never one of those girls that dreams of my wedding day. I just wanted to marry Cyrus, so we went to the courthouse the next day and I love that we did."

"Girl, I don't blame you," Maia says. "Planning a wedding is stressful as hell!"

"Mama is gonna kill you, you know that right," Tiffany says.

"Why do you think I told you before her," Cass says. "I need backup!"

We all burst out laughing.

****

Launch days are some of my favorite days, the excitement of releasing new things and all of the hard work finally coming to fruition. January and February are notoriously known to be the worst months in sales, but we opted for a February release anyway for the items that we weren't able to get in time for our holiday sales and as a nice nod to Valentine's Day.

But launch days also always make me extra nervous too. So many things, always circling through my brain the morning of launch that I have to fight to not have control of my thoughts.

Did I schedule all the social media posts that I needed to?

Did we do enough promotion before today?

Will we meet our sales goal?

Do we have enough inventory?

Do we have too much inventory?

I triple check to make sure the social media posts I have scheduled are good to go, exactly what I want them to be, and then shut my laptop and stand from my desk.

I need a break.

Everything is scheduled and ready to go for the launch, so I decide to take my lunch a little earlier than I normally would and get out of the office.

The weather outside is finally not so briskly cold so I walk the few blocks down the street to my favorite coffee shop. The bell on the door chimes as I step through the front door and I'm instantly greeted by the heavenly scent of coffee and pastries. It's not very busy, the usual afternoon rush is still a few hours away and I'm grateful for the calm of the shop. It's exactly what I need.

I walk up to the counter to order and the owner, Cheyenne, comes from the kitchen in the back. Her signature red locs pulled into a bun on top of her head.

"Hey darling, what can I get for you?" Cheyenne asks with a smile

I look at the pastry case with a frown, noticing that their most popular item, the cinnamon rolls, are sold out. "Damn, I was hoping I got here early enough for a cinnamon roll."

Cinnamon & Spice is known all over town for their delicious handmade cinnamon rolls, so much so that if you come in the morning there's usually a line out the door of people wanting to buy a cinnamon roll with their morning coffee. Cheyenne bakes them throughout the day, refilling the pastry case, but there's still no guarantee that there will be any when you come in due to the high demand.

"If you have some time, I have a fresh batch coming out in about 30 minutes."

I let out a sigh of relief. "Yes that works perfectly, I'll pay for them now and come get them before I leave."

I order a vanilla latte and a chicken pesto panini to have for lunch and cinnamon rolls for me and everyone else at *Lovely Day* as a launch day sweet treat.

My favorite booth is the one tucked in the corner by the front window and thankfully it's available.

Less than five minutes later, Cheyenne brings my coffee and panini over to me at my table. I do a little bit of people watching while I eat my sandwich and drink my coffee, staring out the front window as people rush by on their way to their next destination. This lunch is everything that I needed it to be. I don't scroll on my phone, or check emails, or any of the things I would usually do , I just let myself relax.

More and more people start to file in to Cinnamon & Spice as the lunch rush starts so I decide it's time to get back to work. I slide out of the booth and go to the front counter to pick up my cinnamon rolls. Cheyenne hands me my box that was already set aside which is great because the pastry case is nearly empty again.

The previously blue sky has turned cloudy and gray and the air smells like rain is very near. I quickly walk back over to *Lovely Day*, narrowly making it in the building before large raindrops begin to fall.

"I got cinnamon rolls," I say in a singsong voice as I walk back into the office. "Cheyenne just made them too so they're fresh."

I stop in my tracks when I see Stella, Cass and Reagan all huddled around Cass' desk with looks of shock and confusion on their faces.

"What's going on?" I ask.

"Have you seen the numbers," Stella asks.

My heart immediately drops. "Nooo, I was at lunch. What's going on y'all are scaring me."

Stella hands her tablet to me and my eyes go wide. Hundreds of items of inventory are down to just a few dozen of each and one of them, the lemon vanilla body butter, is already sold out."

"How is this even possible? It's only been like an hour?"

I walk over to my own desk setting down the box of cinnamon rolls and shrugging out of my coat, tossing it over my chair. I pick up my tablet, navigating to our inventory, confident that there was just something wrong with Stella's numbers.

There had to be because what other answer was there.

Right there on my own tablet are the same numbers that were on Stella's. Actually less since every time the inventory refreshes the number of available stock continues to dwindle.

I close out of the inventory and go to Lovely Day's Instagram and I am bombarded by the amount of notifications that have accumulated both from comments on the launch day post and story tags. I go to the comments of the post and there's comment after comment tagging Bryce.

Just placed my order @Sonny

Can't wait to try this out! @Sonny

@Sonny influenced me!

And on and on and on.

I navigate to Bryce's page and right there in his story is a post from a few minutes before the launch. It's a picture of him holding the jar of lemon vanilla body butter with the view of the sky mid-flight as the background. The caption is simply 'the best' with *Lovely Day* tagged.

"How does he even have a jar of the new body butter already? We didn't do any PR boxes for this launch, right?" Cass asks.

I didn't notice her come up behind me, but she takes the tablet from my hands and studies the photo.

"No, we decided against PR boxes this time because we just did them with the holiday launch," Reagan says.

"Sooo," I say, dragging out the word.

Three sets of eyes turn to look at me and I feel like the temperature in the room has been raised tenfold. My heart races as I start to speak, my words coming out fast as I try to explain.

"Remember that time when you asked me to come get the shipment of inventory that I was getting delivered?"

"Yeah, but what does that have to do with anything?" Cass replies.

"Well I was with Bryce, um Sonny, and he offered to bring me and I gave him a tour of the office and then we started talking about my favorite products so I gave him one of the body butter samples we had."

Cass starts to pace, the click of her heels echoing through the room, each step making me more anxious about whatever she's going to say.

"I didn't think it was a big deal and I didn't know that he was going to post about it," I rush to add.

I cringe when Cass starts to speak, worried that she's going to be pissed at me for doing something like that without asking first. She opens and closes her mouth twice, unable to get the words out. Cass pivots on her heel, walks up to me, and pulls me in to a tight hug.

We pull apart and she holds on to my shoulders and finally speaks. "This is amazing!"

"Wait, so you're not mad at me?" I ask, shocked.

"This is the best launch day that *Lovely Day* has ever had," Cass says, dropping her hands and going back to pacing. "And all from just one damn post. Imagine what would happen if..."

I tune the rest of what she says out, my head spinning about what the actual fuck is happening.

"We just sold out of everything!" Reagan says from across the room.

"Girls, it's time to get to packing!" Cass says excitedly.

Cass, Stella and Reagan start walking to the warehouse where the packing station is set up.

"I'll be there in one minute," I call out to them.

I take my phone out of my pocket and FaceTime Bryce. I tap my foot as I wait for the call to connect, on the very last ring he finally answers.

"You were not supposed to post about it," I whisper yell at him.

"Post about what?"

"The body butter! You posted it and now everything is out of stock and it's only been like two hours!"

Bryce smiles, clearly amused. "You're cute as hell when you're mad. Your pretty face all scrunched up."

I ignore the compliment, focusing on my frustration and not the little somersault my belly just did at his words. "This is not funny!"

"Laila, " Bryce says calmly. "I'm sorry I posted about it without telling you. The body butter you gave me is amazing, for real, and I wanted to share it with other people cause I know they'll fuck with it too. I should have given you a heads up first and that's on me, but this is a good thing right?"

"Yes, but that's not the point," I try to argue.

"I'm sorry to do this but I really gotta go. I promise I'll call you later, aight?" Bryce says as someone in the background calls his name. "Oh and don't be mad about the flowers."

The call disconnects before I can respond and not even a minute later the doorbell to the building is buzzing with someone at it. I walk over to the intercom to see who it is. I didn't think we had any packages coming, but with the way today is going, anything is possible.

"Hello?"

"I have a delivery for Laila Eden," a chipper male voice replies.

I buzz him in the building and wait for him to come up the elevator. When the elevator doors open I see the flowers first. A beautiful bouquet of pink peonies.

"Laila Eden?"

"That's me," I reply.

The man hands the vase of flowers to me and gets back on the elevator. The vase is surprisingly heavy so I walk back into the office and set it down on my desk, pushing the long forgotten box of cinnamon rolls out of the way.

I cradle one of the peonies in my fingers, in awe of the beauty of the perfectly formed petals and then I see the card, nestled in the middle of the flowers. I pick it up and open it to read the message inside.

> *If no one else has given you your flowers for*
> *all your hard work, allow me to be the first.*
> *You've done an amazing job and*
> *I hope it's everything you want and more.*
> *-B*

13
Sonny

I'm not nervous.

If anything, I'm the opposite.

Calm, relaxed, maybe even a little excited.

Dez gathers his crew together before the start of the show to do his usual pre show ritual, prayer and shots. We stand in a circle, shoulder to shoulder, and Dez leads the prayer, giving thanks for the opportunity to perform and the blessings that have come our way. At the end we all raise our shot glasses, filled with his signature liquor, and down the contents.

The first stop of this tour is Baltimore, Dez's hometown. Then up and down the east coast before he continues on to the rest of the country over a three month timespan. I was shocked to hear that Dez wanted me to join him on tour, but even more shocked that he wanted me to kick it off with him. The first few stops on a tour really set the tone for how the rest of the dates will go. To be asked was an honor and so I couldn't turn it down, much to everyone's surprise.

I spend the last bit of my time before I go onstage, alone. A moment of quiet, provided by my noise canceling headphones and the last bit of the hot tea that I requested. I take a few deep breaths to get my mind right, sliding the headphones off and setting them down on the table in front of me. Then I stand and exit the dressing room.

The energy in the arena is something I can't even begin to explain, but the feeling sinks into my bones, welcoming me back like an old friend. The bass of the music, the feelings of anticipation running through my veins, the roar of the crowd all of it blending together, welcoming me back with a warm embrace.

I take my place still hidden from view as Dez finishes his song and then begins my introduction.

"Let me see if y'all remember this one," Dez says to the crowd as the first notes of the next song plays.

Dez starts the song out alone, singing the first verse and chorus and then I join him. I start to sing the beginning of my verse, walking slowly out onstage. The intensity and energy of the crowd grows as they realize the surprise and start to sing along.

The crowd is a blur of swaying bodies and lights from people's phones as they record the performance. We keep singing together, dancing and moving around the stage, engaging with the audience until the end of the song.

"Y'all ready for some more?" Dez asks the crowd, holding out his mic to them.

They respond with loud cheers as the next song starts to play.

He gives a wicked smile. "Aight, let's get it."

The high of walking off the stage is unreal. I'm giddy and out of breath, but so damn happy. We performed two more songs and the vibes of the music reminded me of my love for music and sharing it with others.

My contract with my previous label and the negative feelings I had about my last tour made me forget about this part. All of the bad overshadowing this, the good. My wildest dreams that became a reality. But now it's time to do them on my own terms.

***

A week later, Xavier drives my truck around the large fountain in the middle of the driveway and parks next to the other luxury vehicles out front. Blue was sent an alert when we went through security at the front of his gated community so he's aware of our presence and opens the front door as Xavier and I get out of the car. I grab my bag from the backseat, sliding it over my shoulder and shutting the door.

"What's good," Blue says in greeting as we walk up the steps to the front door.

We dap each other up and I step inside the foyer taking in Blue's mansion. He leads us through a large, two story living room and through a hallway to a door that leads down to his basement.

I let out a low whistle. "We ain't in the hood no more huh?"

"A whole lot has changed, that's for sure," Blue says, a cocky smile on his face.

Blue was the first person I ever recorded music with. He had a home studio and would work with the guys in the neighborhood before he started working in an actual studio. Me and some of my friends from back then would pool our money together to pay for studio time because none of us could afford the cost on our own.

When I reached out to set up some recording time with Blue he told me that he had a home studio, but I wasn't expecting a setup this grand. The walls are painted a dark gray and have soundproofing all over them. There's a pool table and a bar on the left side with a mini fridge. Off to the right are couches and a large TV.

On a platform in the middle of the room is a large table filled with monitors, mixing equipment, and TVs. The recording booth is right in front of it with a large window for the engineer and person recording to be able to see each other.

"I do some things here and there, but my days of grinding hard are behind me," Blue says. "But we go way back so you know I got you, whatever you need."

"I appreciate you for making time," I say, taking a seat on one of the couches by the booth.

Blue sits in the chair in front of the mixing desk.

"Do you have something specific in mind already or did you just want to vibe and see where things go?"

"A little of both. I have a couple tracks I want to put down for sure, but other than that we can just see where things take us."

"Cool," Blue says, tapping some things out on his computer keyboard. "Send me what you have and we can go from there."

I send him all the files and I see them all brought up on the TV screen in front of us. Dozens of files. Most of it is just beats, the lyrics written down in my writing journal in my bag. But a few of them are voice recordings, nothing fancy, just me singing as I play the piano.

"Where do you want to start?"

I point to one of the files on the screen. "Here."

Blue clicks on it and is about to start it when I interject. "It's different from anything I've done before."

Blue presses a button and the track starts, all piano at first.

"Acoustic?" Blue says, raising a brow in surprise.

I just nod, sitting back on the couch and listening to the rest of the song. As the last notes play I look over at Blue and try to gauge his feelings on the song. This is the first time that anyone else has heard anything new that I've written, and I know that Blue will give it to me straight.

Blue brings his hand up to his face, rubbing his chin and I can see the gears turning in his head.

"Damn, you weren't lying when you said it was different," Blue says finally.

"I want to make something that feels like me," I reply.

"And this does that for you?"

I nod.

Slowly a smile crosses over his face. "This is probably the best song I've ever heard from you. Let's get to work."

14
Laila

My phone ringing jolts me awake. I had been in bed editing content for *Lovely Day*'s social media platforms when I must have fallen asleep. It's dark in my room, the only light sources coming from my tv and my open laptop next to me in my bed.

I reach out to my nightstand and grab my phone to see Bryce FaceTiming me. I answer the phone still snuggled under my blankets.

"Hello?" I say, yawning.

"I'm sorry, I didn't mean to wake you. I didn't think you'd be asleep already."

Usually I wouldn't be, I'm notorious for always being up at all times of night working. Today I had been tired all day and despite trying to push through it, my body clearly had other plans.

Something in Bryce's voice is off, his usual nonchalant, teasing personality is absent and instead he's quiet. I haven't seen him in person since he came back from Baltimore because we both have been busy.

"What's wrong?" I ask my brows knit with worry.

"Nothing," he replies. "I shouldn't have called, get some sleep."

I don't believe him. He's in the car with the phone resting in his lap. Instead of seeing his face I see the headliner of his car and the front windshield, street lights passing by as he drives. But even without seeing his face I can just tell that something is really bothering him.

I sit up in my bed. "Bryce, tell me what's wrong."

He lets out a deep sigh. "Do you want to take a drive with me?"

"Yeah, okay."

"Bet. I'll be there in a few."

Bryce ends the FaceTime and I sit in my bed confused about what's happening for a minute. My brain goes down a long list of possibilities for what's going on with him and I have to force myself to stop speculating.

My phone chimes with a new text message.

sonny

I'm here

He got here much quicker than I expected him to, but I quickly get out of bed and gather myself together to meet him downstairs.

An orange Hellcat Charger is parked in the fire lane in front of my building, it's hazard lights flashing. Bryce is leaning against the car dressed in all black sweats and a fitted White Sox hat pulled low onto his head to shade his face from being recognized by anyone who may walk by.

"Hey," I say softly.

Bryce doesn't say anything, he just takes my hand and gently pulls me forward into a hug. He wraps his arms around me and I'm completely immersed in the warmth of him and it feels like I melt against his body. We stay in the hug until Bryce pulls away.

"This you?" I ask, tilting my head towards the car.

This car is unfamiliar to me. Every time I've seen Bryce's car, it's been the same black SUV so this is a stark difference.

"Yeah, this is my baby. I just pulled her out of storage."

"Her?" I say. "Don't tell me she has a name too."

"Of course she does," he replies, opening the passenger door for me to get in.

I slide in and Bryce closes the door behind me before he walks around the front of the car to get into the driver's seat. He left the car running so he shifts the car from park to drive and just drives.

Five minutes pass.

And then ten.

And then twenty.

And still Bryce just drives.

He drives with seemingly no real destination in mind. Music plays quietly through the car speakers but Bryce doesn't say anything. I watch his side profile, the set of his jaw, the curve of his nose, the fullness of his lips. Unabashedly cataloging all of him.

I'm bubbling with the need to know what's bothering him, what's making him so sad but I'm trying to give him the space to share it on his own, whatever it is.

At the next red light Bryce merges into the left lane and puts his turn signal on. The light turns green and he takes the turn merging onto Lake Shore Drive. I look out the window and out into the pitch dark of Lake Michigan, a stark contrast to the bright lights of the city to our left.

"Ask me."

"What?" I reply, confused.

"Ask me whatever is on your mind," he says.

"Are you okay?"

"No," he murmurs. "But I will be."

I take his free hand that had been resting on the arm rest into mine, sliding my fingers into the free spaces between his and covering it with my other hand.

"It's been almost five years since I lost my dad," he says, turning to look at me for a second. "The last time I saw him was right there, right where you're sitting."

My stomach drops hearing the pain laced through his words and even more so as he continues.

"My sister Shannon was the one who called me with the news. I didn't know it at the time because no one told me, but his health was rapidly declining. He wasn't that old and was seemingly healthy until he wasn't. The doctor's didn't figure it out until it was too late, the cancer diagnosis coming only a short while before he passed."

"I'm sorry Bryce."

I say the words and I mean them but they don't feel like enough, they aren't enough because there aren't any words that you can say that can mend the pain of losing a parent.

"The day my sister called me, I flew home to be with my mom and my sisters for his funeral. But I couldn't stay home for long because two weeks later was the start of my tour and no one gave a damn that I had just lost my dad. They didn't care that I felt like a piece of me had died with him. They only cared about me getting on the stage and performing damn near every night. So I did. And life just continued, the world kept spinning."

Bryce rubs his hand across the steering wheel. "I bought this car when I made my first real money as a singer. It was my dream car at the time and I bought it brand new off the lot. My first brand new car."

I stay quiet and let Bryce talk and rub my thumb over the back of his hand to let him know I'm listening.

"My mom was pissed," he continues with a sad chuckle. "She said I was wasting money and I shouldn't be out 'spending it all crazy'. But my dad understood. He was so fucking proud."

A tear slides down Bryce's cheek, followed quickly by more and I reach over and gently brush them away with the pad of my thumb.

"I bet he still is," I say softly.

Bryce nods.

"Is there anything I can do?" I whisper.

Bryce gives my hand a quick squeeze. "You're doing it."

"You sure?"

"Yeah," he replies. "Driving has always been my way of clearing my head, but tonight I wanted to see you and you came. So yes, this is enough."

Bryce turns up the music and returns his hand to hold mine and we just keep driving.

I don't last much longer before my eyes get heavy and the lull of the car sends me to sleep. When I open my eyes again Bryce is nudging me awake. We're parked in his parking spot in the garage under his building.

"Stay with me tonight."

Bryce says the words as a statement and I don't fight him on it.

"Okay," I reply with a yawn.

I unbuckle my seatbelt and get out of the car following Bryce into the building and into the elevator to go up to his condo. Bryce holds his key fob to the reader and presses the button for his floor and the elevator doors close.

Bryce tugs on the strings of the hoodie I threw on when I changed out of my pajamas. "This looks familiar."

I look down and realize in my haste to meet him outside my apartment I grabbed the hoodie he gave me the first time we met. Since we've become friends, I've taken a couple more of Bryce's hoodies, but this one has remained my favorite of them all.

"Yeah?" I reply. "I stole it from a friend. I think it looks better on me though."

He gives me a small smile, the first one I've seen from him all night and my heart constricts at the sight of it.

"I think so too."

The elevator doors open and we walk into the condo.

"Let me get you something to sleep in," Bryce says, walking to his bedroom.

In his room he goes to his dresser, pulling open a couple of drawers and taking out a pair of pajama pants and a t-shirt.

I take them from him, escaping to the bathroom to change. The shirt is soft, the kind of soft where you can tell it's been worn a million times and has gone through the washing machine just as many. I leave my clothes in a folded pile on the counter for me to change back into in the morning and leave the bathroom to go to the living room. I don't make it far down the hallway before I hear Bryce behind me.

"Where are you going?"

I turn around and see him walking towards me until he's less than an arms length away.

"To the couch," I reply, confused by his confusion

"Nah pretty girl," he says, shaking his head. "Take the bed, I'll take the couch."

"No, I don't want to kick you out of your own bed. I can take the couch."

"Laila."

"Why do you have to be so difficult?"

"I'm not being difficult," he replies. "I want you to have the bed and you want me to have it so where does that leave us?"

I let out a deep sigh. "We can share."

"Share?"

"Share," I repeat. "The bed is big enough and then no one has to sleep on the couch."

"Fine, we can have it your way but you have to promise me one thing."

"And what's that?" I ask.

Bryce takes a step closer and my breath catches. His eyes stare into mine and the pounding of my heart makes me want to look away but I can't.

"Stop doubting that I want you around, because I do. You aren't a burden or an inconvenience and fuck whoever made you feel like you are."

***

I was so tired the night before I don't remember falling asleep. One minute I was climbing into Bryce's extra plush bed and then... nothing. I rub my eyes in an attempt to clear away the remnants of sleep and sit up in the bed.

The space next to me where I expected Bryce to be is empty. I climb out of the bed in search of my phone when I realize that it isn't on the nightstand. Exhaustion must have really been kicking my ass last night because I hadn't even thought about putting my phone on the charger or setting my alarms, I just went right to sleep.

I find my phone in the pocket of my pants that I left in the bathroom. I try to turn it on but a blank screen stares back at me when I push the button.

"Great," I mutter, annoyed that I forgot to charge it.

I walk back into the bedroom in search of a charger and find one on Bryce's side of the bed. I plug my phone in and wait for it to turn on. When it does it immediately begins to ding with a bunch of notifications. Emails, text messages, social media comments, and direct messages. Then I see the time, a full three hours past the time that I intended to wake up.

"Shit," I curse to myself.

I leave my phone charging and go in search of Bryce, padding down the hall to the living room. Movement on the balcony catches my eye and I see Bryce sitting out there on a small couch with his back to me. He's scribbling things in a leather journal, head bent in concentration.

I walk over and pull open one of the french doors, the early spring air is cooler than I anticipated based on Bryce's lack of clothing.

Bryce looks up from his notebook and smiles at me. "Hey sleepyhead."

"Why didn't you wake me?"

"You were tired so I let you sleep," he says. "Snoring too."

"I don't snore!" I exclaim.

Bryce chuckles and pats beside him for me to come over and sit.

"No, I probably smell. I haven't showered or brushed my teeth or anything yet."

"I didn't ask you about any of that. Come here."

With a huff I comply, closing the few steps of distance between us. He sets his notebook and pen on the small table next to us and then turns his attention back to me.

"Did you sleep well?" he asks.

"I was supposed to be up hours ago. I forgot to set an alarm."

"That's not what I asked you."

"Why are you being difficult?" I ask.

"I'm not," he says simply. "I asked about how you slept, that's what I care about. Not what time you were 'supposed' to be awake."

I roll my eyes at him and frown.

"You can pout all you want. I care about you, not your productivity."

"I actually slept great," I concede.

"I bet you did," he replies, mimicking snoring noises.

I playfully smack his chest. "I do not snore!"

I fold my legs under me to sit criss-cross and lean my shoulder against Bryce's.

"How are you?" I ask softly.

Bryce being vulnerable and sharing his grief with me last night isn't something I want to gloss over or minimize because it's a big deal. Of all the people he could've gone to last night he chose me and I want to honor that. To hold space for his feelings, for his grief, because he deserves it.

"I'm okay," he replies. "Grief is a bitch sometimes. It's been years so I guess it shouldn't hurt as much anymore, but it does."

"There's no timeline for when you should be done grieving the loss of someone you love. Despite what they say, time doesn't heal all wounds."

"Thank you," he murmurs, wrapping an arm around me.

"For what?"

"For being here."

"You don't have to thank me for that. It's no big deal."

"It is a big deal," he says. "I literally woke you up out of your sleep and you were here when I needed you. That's a big deal to me."

I turn so I can see Bryce's face fully and when I do I can see the sincerity in his eyes. My heart swells at the gratitude displayed so prominently all over his face and I can feel all the emotions that I've held back, pushed down and closed behind the door of 'friendship' clawing to fight their way out.

My stomach grumbles, loudly, and we both burst out laughing at the intrusion.

Bryce taps my thigh, signaling for me to stand up, I do and he follows. "Come on, let's get you some food."

"That's okay, I'll eat when I get home. I'm already really behind on the things I need to get done."

"Do you have anything due today? Anything that is an absolute necessity that you do?" he asks.

"Well no, but I-"

"Eat first," he says, cutting me off, standing to his full height. "And then I'll take you home. The work will still be there after you eat."

"Are you holding me hostage?" I ask looking up at him.

"Is that what you want to call it? Correct me if I'm wrong but I don't think hostages get breakfast made for them in a penthouse in the city."

Bryce opens the door and holds it open for me to walk through first and I don't bother protesting anymore. My stomach was growling again at the mention of food again, impatiently insisting that I remedy its emptiness pronto.

I take a seat in one of the stools at the island and watch Bryce move around in the kitchen, opening cabinets and drawers and pulling things out.

"You're making food for me?" I ask, surprised.

Bryce chuckles at my question before answering. "I am. Is that okay?"

I watch as he pulls out a carton of eggs and some bacon amongst other ingredients. "Yeah of course, I just didn't expect it, that's all. I figured that you would have people for these kinds of things. A chef or something."

"I do have a chef, but I tend to fend for myself for breakfast because I don't really like rewarmed breakfast foods. And my mom made sure I knew how to cook. She wasn't having any of that gender roles in the household shit."

I nod in understanding. "

"What about you?" he asks. "Do you cook?"

"I mean I *can* cook, like I won't starve or anything. I just don't really like cooking, I don't find joy in it the way that other people do."

Bryce nods his head in understanding and I watch as he cracks a couple of eggs into a bowl in preparation to scramble them.

"Is there any food that you don't like?"

"Tomatoes," I reply, crinkling my nose.

"Tomatoes," Bryce repeats. "Got it."

Bryce finishes making us breakfast and places a fully assembled plate in front of me before he joins me at the island with a plate of his own. When it comes to types of foods, breakfast foods rank amongst my least favorites. I would happily eat a burrito or a bowl of pasta at the crack of dawn without a care in the world that

I wasn't eating 'breakfast' food. But the breakfast Bryce makes, while simple, is exactly how I would want it to be made. The pancakes have the slight crunchy edge that I love and the bacon is at the exact right cook and my scrambled eggs aren't too hard or too runny, because sometimes runny eggs make my stomach turn, and then I can't eat them. Bryce didn't know any of this; he just made me breakfast, yet somehow I wouldn't change a thing. As he promised, after we eat, we put our dishes in the sink and Bryce takes me back home.

15
Laila

"THIS SPACE IS AMAZING," Cass says, spinning in a slow circle in the empty warehouse.

This is the fourth space we've seen today and I couldn't agree more. It's in a great location, still close to downtown Rosewood, and most of the updates that we would have wanted are already done. The only thing we would have to do is some small customizations to make it exactly what we need. Cass already wanted to expand and then this past launch went so well that she really started to put everything in motion to find *Lovely Day* a bigger location.

"This location just came up for lease this week so it hasn't been seen by very many people yet. So if you want it I would suggest we put in a contract sooner rather than later, so no one else gets it," says Rose, the realtor.

"What do you think?" Cass asks, looking at me.

"I think it's beautiful and everything we were looking for. You should do it."

Rose's phone rings. "I'm going to step out to take this call."

Her heels echo across the hardwood floors as she walks to the exit until it's just me and Cass left inside.

"This place has room for over double the inventory of what we usually hold, so hopefully we can keep things in stock better," Cass says.

I hum in agreement, already having a suspicion that this conversation was going in a direction that I didn't want it to.

"Once we fulfill all the preorders, I'm thinking we should have way more stock for the next launch. You know, since the last one did so well."

I cut my eyes to her and see the fake innocent smile on her face.

"What are you thinking for paint colors? Cream maybe?" I ask, deflecting.

"You really aren't going to give me any details about you and him?"

"Maybe darker, like a beige could be nice," I say, walking over to one of the large oversized windows. "The lighting is fantastic, and beige could be a great neutral for photos."

Cass doesn't respond. When I turn to face her, her arms are crossed over her chest.

"Please," she says, dragging out the word. "Just give me something."

"What do you want to know?" I ask.

"Anything. Everything! You dropped the bomb about knowing him on release day and then never said anything else. You must be close because you wouldn't have brought just anyone to the office."

"There isn't much to tell."

"Fine, how about how you even met him?"

I tell her the story, from meeting each other years ago to literally accidentally running into each other again a few months ago.

"Wow that's a real life meet cute!" Cass says.

"But we're just friends."

"Is this where I'm supposed to just add in the 'with benefits' part or?"

"No!" I say, laughing. "I'm serious, we really do just talk. We spend a lot of time together at his place, watching tv or movies."

I leave out the part about how much my body involuntarily reacts to his presence and how talking with him, even for a short while, is the highlight of my day. Because none of that matters.

We're. Just. Friends.

"Mhmmm," Cass says, disbelief in her tone.

"It's true. You were there for everything that happened with Devin, I'm not ready to go through something like that again. Especially someone that's as well known as Bry-, I mean Sonny, is."

Cass notices my slip up, but doesn't acknowledge it.

"You're right, I was there for Devin," Cass says. "But what happened with Devin isn't going to happen again. You can't give up on finding love just because of one ain't shit nigga."

"Love? Nobody said anything about love."

"Girl, he sold out our entire inventory and sent you flowers unprompted on release day. He may not be in love now, but he damn sure could be if you gave him a chance."

"Just because the chance worked for you doesn't mean it will for me," I argue back. "We're just friends."

"For now," Cass says, her tone serious as if it's already a foregone conclusion that Bryce and I will end up together.

"Anyway," Cass says, shifting the conversation. "I wanted to ask you if you thought that he would be interested in doing any promotional work with *Lovely Day*?"

I chew on my bottom lip. "I don't know. Are you sure that's something you'd want to do?"

"If he truly loves the product as much as he said that he did it would be great to do some actual promotional work with him. It's one thing to seek someone out to try a product and give a review but for them to authentically like it on their own is even better."

"That's true," I reply, hesitantly.

"We could do a photoshoot and have some small videos as well. We haven't done one of those in forever and you're so good at them."

Cass gets a far away look in her eyes as she talks and I can tell she's planning and organizing in her head at a million miles a minute. Cass loves to plan and once she gets started she's all in.

My phone buzzes and I reach into my purse to grab it. I shake my head at the fucking coincidence when I see the name that is on the screen.

"It's him isn't it," Cass says with a little squeal. "I'll give you a minute to talk. I'm going to go tell Rose to get started on the paperwork."

"Your ears were burning huh?" I say in reference to him calling while I was talking about him.

"You were talking about me?" he asks, a grin coming to his face. "All good things I hope."

"Something like that. We just finished looking at the new warehouse location

"Y'all found one you like? That's amazing."

"Yeah it's pretty great and has everything we were looking for."

"Now tell me why you were talking about me," Bryce says.

"We were talking and you just came up," I wave my hand in the air to signify the insignificance of it.

"Bullshit," he says, calling my bluff.

I sigh dramatically.

"Well, since someone decided to post about *Lovely Day*," I say with a fake stern look. "It left people with questions."

"I'm sorry, I didn't think about how it would draw attention from the people you work with."

"It's fine, I know you didn't mean any harm," I reply. "But my boss did want me to ask you something."

"Go for it."

My heart rate rises as I gather my words, nervous to speak them aloud for some reason.

My words come out rushed and jumbled together. "My boss, well she's my friend too, she wanted me to ask you something. But I should've just told her no because it's dumb to even ask and -"

"Laila," Bryce says softly, interrupting my rambling.

"Yeah?"

"Tell me what you need from me, pretty girl."

I let out another sigh. This time to try to quell the nerves and anxiety of asking the question.

Once I've fully gathered myself I speak again. "Cass wants to know if you'd be interested in working with *Lovely Day*."

"Yes."

I don't hear his response and instead keep rambling until I catch myself. "It wouldn't have to be anything elaborate, or over the top and... wait, what did you say?"

A smile is back on his face, the amusement shining in his deep brown eyes. "I said yes."

"Why?"

"Did you want me to say no?" Bryce asks

"Well no," I reply. "But I thought that you would want more details, or even to see a contract, or pricing, or something before agreeing."

"I want to do it because you asked me. And if posing for a picture and telling people about something I genuinely like will benefit you, I'm going to do it every time. Morgan can worry about the contract."

"Oh," I reply, simply, at a loss for words.

My chest warms at his words and we sit in silence for a moment as I process until Bryce speaks again.

"I was calling you because I know we said we would start the new season of the show, but I'm still in the studio and I'm probably going to be here for a while."

"That's okay, I'm about to head back to the office anyway. We still have a bunch of things to do since the preorder inventory is starting to arrive," I say.

"Let me know when you get home safe tonight, okay?"

I nod. "Okay."

16
Sonny

Laila lays across my couch, cuddled under a blanket that has gained a permanent spot on the back of my couch since she's always cold when we're watching tv. Her feet are resting on top of my thighs. The comfortable routine that we've fallen into every time she comes over.

After a week in Baltimore, I was more than ready to be home. I was finally ready to formally make music again which led to the studio session with Blue, but this is what I was most looking forward to getting back to.

Back to my routine. Back to … Laila.

We spent time on FaceTime while I was away, but the thing I missed most was the days spent with her doing the simplest things like watching her favorite show.

"Oooo I love this episode," Laila says after the theme song plays.

I learned very early on to *never* try to skip the theme song for this show. I did once one of the first times we watched the show together and you would have thought I kicked a puppy by the look of betrayal on Laila's face. Now we listen to the song every single time and Laila hums or sings along. I've even found myself doing the same from time to time.

"You say that about every episode," I say, teasing.

"I know, but I really love this one."

My phone buzzes loudly drawing both our attention to where it sits on the kitchen counter.

"You don't want to get that?" Laila asks when I don't make any move to get up.

"Nah, it's probably nothing and if it is they'll call back."

Truthfully I'm just not in the mood to talk to anyone. After coming back from performing with Dez in Baltimore, it's felt like everyone has wanted something from me.

News outlets want statements, or interviews about the performance, and what I'm up to. Essence reaching out more to get me on her album. Even Dez asking me to come back out for more stops on his tour because the buzz has been so crazy. So many questions that I really don't have the answer for.

Does this mean you're back?

Are you going to do more performances?

When's your next album coming out?

So many questions.

The quiet, simplicity that I had just a few weeks ago now nonexistent. I had to tell Morgan to stop telling me about everything that's been going on because I just don't have the answers.

Everything combined has put so much more on my plate and I don't even know where to begin.

Laila waves a hand in front of my face, trying to get my attention. I hadn't realized I was zoned out, battling with all the things in my head but when I look up at the tv, the show is paused halfway through the episode.

"My bad, what did you say?" I say, focusing my eyes on Laila.

She has on one of my hoodies that she stole out of my closet, something that has become a frequent habit of hers when we watch tv on my couch. They usually end up leaving with her but in the small chance that she leaves them, her lemon and vanilla scent clings to the fabric reminding me of her even in her absence.

"What's got you zoned out?"

"Thinking about the meeting I had with that label."

Laila scrunches her nose. Performing with Dez made me realize that I wanted to get back into music sooner rather than later and so I decided to take a couple of meetings with labels. I filled Laila in on the most recent meeting while we split a cinnamon roll from her favorite place, so she knows exactly how terribly that encounter went.

"Everything feels the same. I've met with so many executives, and so many labels, but it all feels like the same bullshit just delivered from a different person. I haven't met anyone that has made me feel like I can trust them with not just my music but me as a human."

"Maybe you just have to trust yourself instead."

My phone starts buzzing again on the counter. It stops and then immediately starts again. I guess that means it's important. I tap Laila's ankle for her to move her feet and when she does I stand to go answer my phone.

"Hello," I say into the phone when I place it against my ear.

"Hey Bryce," Lauryn says.

"What's wrong?" I ask immediately.

Lauryn never calls me 'Bryce', I can't even remember the last time she's used my first name. It's always 'B' or baby bro, or even Sonny, but never Bryce.

She doesn't say anything for a minute and my worry and impatience grows.

"Lauryn?"

"Mommy is in the hospital," Lauryn says, her voice quiet and quivering on the last word.

My vision goes blurry as I try to process Lauryn's words but I can't. I can't understand because it can't be true.

I place my free hand down on to the edge of the counter to brace myself, my entire body going numb.

"What?" I croak.

I hear Lauryn take in a deep breath, trying to contain her own emotions, before she speaks again. "Shannon called Mommy's phone but she didn't answer. She called again and a nurse answered her phone and said she was in the hospital but she didn't give any more information. I have to go pick up RJ from the sitter and –"

I don't hear the rest of Lauryn's sentence, the words fading into the background noise of my brain. The pain in my chest rises as the eerie sense of deja vu heightens as I remember the last time one of my sisters and I were on a call so similar to this one.

"What hospital?"

Hearing that, Laila turns around on the couch and looks at me with concern written all over her face.

"Shannon didn't want me to tell you because she doesn't want you to worry and I'm on my way there already."

"What hospital, Lauryn?" I ask, frustrated that even now as a grown ass man, they're treating me like a kid who only gets little bits and pieces of information.

"Jasper Heights."

I pull the phone away from my face and end the call, dropping the phone onto the counter next to me I squeeze my eyes closed, trying desperately to get my rapidly beating heart to slow down.

I feel Laila's presence when she comes up next to me. Her signature lemon and vanilla scent infiltrating my nostrils and offering my body an ounce of calm and reprieve from my mind that was set on conjuring up every worst case scenario.

Scenarios that I hope with every fiber of my being aren't true. They can't be true.

"Breathe," Laila says softly.

I inhale deeply, holding it for a moment and then exhaling before repeating the process several more times. Through the cotton of my t-shirt I feel Laila rub my back in slow comforting circles.

"I have to go to the hospital," I whisper.

"Then let's go."

***

I stare at the numbers on the elevator as they climb, feeling like they're moving in slow motion. The entire drive to the hospital felt so much longer than the actual half an hour it took to get here.

Laila steps closer to me and slides her hand into mine, her palm soft as her fingers entwine perfectly with mine. She gives my hand a gentle, reassuring squeeze. I look from our hands to her face and give a small half smile that I hope conveys how grateful I am that she's here with me.

The elevator finally stops and the door slides open. We follow the signs in the hallway towards the room number the hospital's receptionist wrote down on the slip of paper that's in my pocket.

415.

As we approach the door opens and my sister Shannon steps out, shutting it softly behind her.

"What's going on, is everything okay?" I ask.

"Mom is fine," Shannon says agitated. "I told Lauryn not to tell you and get you all worried."

"Get me all worried?" I echo back frustrated and confused. "What else should I be when I get a call that our mom is in the fucking hospital."

The words come out louder than I intended and a nurse walking by gives me a side eye.

"See, this is exactly why I didn't want you to know."

"And that's for you to decide?" I counter.

Shannon cuts her eyes at Laila beside me.

"Can I talk to you?" she asks before turning to Laila and directing her next word to her. "Alone."

"What is your problem?" I ask, confused at the unwarranted hostility.

Shannon frowns and crosses her arms over her chest.

"No, it's fine," Laila says. "I was going to go to the bathroom anyway."

Laila takes her hand out of mine and steps away from me and Shannon. I want to argue back, to tell her that she doesn't have to go anywhere. Tell her that I want her to be right where she is, but before I can get any words out she's stepping away walking down the hall to the nurses station. The station is too far away for me to hear the nurse's response, but she points down a hallway and Laila walks in that direction until she turns a corner out of my view.

"Why would you bring her here?" Shannon asks.

Her tone laced with such contempt, that it draws my eyes away from Laila and to my sister.

"Really? That's the first thing you want to say to me right now?" I ask, shaking my head in disbelief. "Mom is in there lying in a hospital room and you want to talk about why I brought Laila?"

"Exactly, mom is in the hospital," Shannon says, her tone harsh. "Which means this is family business, not somewhere where you bring your little fuck buddy to."

Shannon is the oldest and has always been the bossiest. She always wants things done her way and thinks that she knows best about everything. Even when she's loud and wrong.

I step closer to Shannon, getting in her space to make sure my next words are crystal clear. "Listen, I get that there's a lot going on right now, but don't you ever say some disrespectful shit like that about Laila ever again. She's here because I want her to be, and that's all that matters."

Shannon's nostrils flare as she prepares to argue back with me but Lauryn's voice from down the hall breaks the tension.

"Hey, sorry, I got here as soon as I could," Lauryn says, coming up beside the two of us. "Fill me in. What's going on?"

"Since Shannon knows everything, she can tell you. I'm going to go see mom," I say.

I don't wait for a response from either of them, I step back and walk to the door of Mom's hospital room. I knock gently before I let myself in.

Janet Taylor is the rock of my family.

The one who has always brought us all together. The one who was at every recital, every orientation, every gameday for her children, cheering us on.

I'm used to her strength and independence. Which makes me so wholly unprepared when I step into her room and see her in a hospital gown, hooked up to an IV and other machines. She's lying against her pillows with her eyes closed and my chest clenches as I take in this version of my mother that I haven't let myself see before.

The show of aging in the form of wrinkles across her forehead. The gray hairs that aren't just at her temples anymore, but are now winning the battle against the dark brown ones throughout her head.

The evidence of her mortality, right in front of my eyes.

"Don't just stand there Bryce, come on over here," my mom says, her eyes still closed.

"How did you know it was me?"

"A mother knows her son."

I do as she says, rounding the bed I place a kiss on her forehead before pulling a visitor's chair closer to the bed so I can sit next to her.

"How you feeling, ma?"

"I'm feeling just fine."

"Ma," I say, my tone serious.

She waves a hand in the air as if to say it's irrelevant but I don't believe her. I fix her with a hard stare until she speaks again.

"The doctor only wants to keep me overnight for observation as a precaution."

"A precaution for what?"

She sighs. "I was having some chest pains and shortness of breath this afternoon. I came in to get it checked out. The doctors said my heart is just fine, but my blood pressure is high and they want to get it under control."

I let out a breath of air, grateful it wasn't something more serious but still concerned nonetheless.

"Under control how?"

"Some medication, some changes to my diet and exercise levels," my mom says, her calm tone a direct antithesis to how I'm feeling. "Unless the man upstairs has other plans, I'm going to be just fine."

"Why didn't you call me? Or any of us?"

"Because I didn't need you, or your sisters, in here fussing over me. You don't have to worry."

"I don't need to worry?" I ask. "Just like I didn't have to worry about dad?"

"Things with your father were different."

"Different how?" I ask, confused. "Because to me, the only thing that's different is that I'm not across the country and can actually be here but still you won't let me."

"Not a day goes by that I don't regret not telling you about your father," my mom says, taking one of my hands in both of hers. "But he didn't want you to know because he wanted you to keep living your dreams. He didn't want you to drop everything."

"But what about what I wanted?" I ask, emotion causing my voice to catch.

My mom squeezes my hands tighter and looks directly into my eyes. The glossiness of her eyes causes the tears that I was barely holding in, to fall, streaking down my face.

"You're right, it wasn't fair and I am so sorry for how that happened. From now on you'll know just as much as your sisters do, okay?"

I nod. "Okay."

My mom releases my hand and lays back in the bed. "Now tell me about how those performances went."

Lauryn and Shannon come in a few minutes into me telling my mom about my time in Baltimore performing with Dez. Shannon slides a chair to the other side of the bed and Lauryn climbs in with mom, sitting cross legged at the foot of the bed.

We all sit and talk, filling our mom in on the things that have happened in our lives since we each saw her last. A nurse comes in to take my mom's vitals and administer her evening medicine, something to help with her high blood pressure. On her way out, the nurse tells us that visiting hours end in 15 minutes, a not so subtle way to tell us to leave.

Shannon stands and gives our Mom a hug, whispering an 'I love you' before quickly leaving.

"What's that all about?" Mom asks as the door closes.

Lauryn looks over in my direction and I just shrug.

"She's upset that B brought his girlfriend," Lauryn says.

"She's not my girlfriend," I say as I stand. "We're just friends, we were together when Lauryn called so she came with me. That's all."

"I want to hear more about this *friend*, next time," my Mom says as I place a kiss on her head and hug her.

"I love you, Mom," I reply, avoiding her statement.

She smiles a mischievous look in her eye. "I love you too."

Lauryn and I leave the room together. We hug goodbye and then go our separate ways, her to her car and me to Laila.

I find her in a nearby waiting room curled up in a chair in the corner, asleep. I gently nudge her arm until her eyes flutter open, squinting at the bright fluorescents shining overhead.

"C'mon, let me take you home," I say, holding my hand out to her.

She accepts my hand and I help her stand and we make our way to the elevators. We step into the elevator and I press the button to take us to the lobby.

"How's your mom?" Laila asks.

"Yeah she's good, they're keeping her overnight, but she's feeling better."

Laila's shoulders visibly relax. "Good, I'm so happy she's okay."

"Thank you for coming with me tonight. It means a lot, truly."

"You're welcome, I didn't want you to have to go alone."

On the ground floor we exit the elevator and make the short walk back to my car. I open the passenger door for Laila, making sure she's safely inside before shutting her door and walking around to my own.

I start the car and exit the parking garage.

"Shit, I left my purse at your place," Laila says a few minutes into the drive. "We left so quickly I didn't remember to grab it."

"No worries, it's closer anyway."

I hit a u-turn and head towards home. The drive that felt so long headed to the hospital now feels short. I press the code to the garage attached to my building and the door opens. I reverse into my parking spot and kill the engine.

"I'll just run up and grab it and then I'll be out of your hair," Laila says unbuckling her seatbelt.

"You don't have to," I say. "Leave I mean. You can stay if you want to."

Laila's teeth sink into her bottom lip as she thinks over the offer. "I don't want to be in your way."

"I wouldn't have offered it if I thought you would be," I say, unbuckling my own seatbelt. "We can even finish that episode you love."

17
Sonny

Morgan is already seated at the table when I arrive for our meeting. She's sitting on the booth side of the table, her tablet attached to a keyboard as she types away.

"Here I was thinking I was getting here early," I joke as I walk up to the table and take my seat across from her.

Morgan looks up at me and smiles. "Not this time. I got here a little bit ago to work on some things before our meeting."

A waiter comes and takes our order and when he leaves Morgan gets right to business.

"So your interests have shifted to working with small beauty brands now?" Morgan asks.

"I've always been interested in working with businesses I align with. Nothing's changed, it just happened to be skin care."

"Interesting."

"Weren't you one of the people telling me to diversify?"

"I was, I just didn't think we'd end up here, but I'm not mad at it."

"So everything's set with that?"

"I made a few suggested changes, but I sent it over to the lawyers to look at it as well. Once they send it back you'll be all set."

"Good, I'm looking forward to it."

Morgan gives me a skeptical look but doesn't press any further with her thoughts and instead changes topics.

"The response to you doing that performance has been great. People still really enjoy you and Dez, and have been asking for more of it."

Our food is delivered to our table and we both shift some of our focus to eating. We talk over the usual things of our check ins, upcoming obligations, new opportunities, and so on. We have just about wrapped up when Morgan gets serious and folds her hands together.

"Last thing."

The way Morgan says it, I know I'm not going to like whatever she says next. I lean back in my chair and nod my head, telling her to go on.

"A record label owner has been reaching out to me to get a meeting with you. His name is Langston St. James with Silver Spoon Records."

"I've never heard of it."

"You probably wouldn't, it's newer and only has about a dozen artists signed. He's called me everyday for the past two weeks trying to get a meeting with you."

"So he's desperate," I say.

"Or persistent."

Over the years I've had a lot of offers to meet with record labels, especially those first few months after leaving my last one. I didn't want to play the game of the industry, the song and dance of begging for a company to care more about you as a person than the hypothetical money they would be losing for having a conscience.

Morgan knows my stance and she agrees so for her to even be bringing this topic up to me is a surprise.

"Why this one?"

"Because we can't do the same thing and expect a different outcome. You love music more than most people love anything. I've witnessed it first hand, and so I know how much of a block it must have been to not create for years while you healed and found yourself again. But for the first time in three years you're recording again, and I'll be damned if I don't put a potentially great opportunity in front of you. Not only because that's what you pay me to do, but also because I care about *you*, Sonny."

This time it's Morgan who sits back in her seat.

I soak in her words, really taking them in and digesting them before I respond.

"Fine. Set it up and I'll be there, but I'm not making any promises."

"I'm not asking you to," Morgan says. "He could be full of shit and I would fully expect you to tell him to kick rocks, respectfully."

***

Three days later I'm walking into Silver Spoon Records to have a meeting with Langston St. James himself. Normally, Morgan would have been a part of a meeting like this but she had a family emergency come up and I opted to take the meeting myself to get it out of the way instead of rescheduling.

When his assistant sees Xavier and I approaching, she immediately stands and gives me an eager smile, welcoming me to the office. Xavier takes a seat on a nearby couch to wait. She walks me to the office door, tapping her knuckles two times on the door before opening it.

"Sonny is here to see you, sir," the assistant says.

Langston stands from his seat behind his desk, shaking my hand with a firm grip. He stands a few inches shorter than me and is younger than I expected, in his late thirties. He's dressed in a black suit, something expensive by the looks of it and sharply contrasting the casual clothes I decided on for this meeting.

"Is there anything I can get for the two of you, Mr. St. James?" his assistant asks. "Sparkling water, tea, coffee?"

Langston looks at me, silently asking if I'm interested in anything. I shake my head.

"No, Michaela, we're fine here," he replies.

Michaela leaves the office, closing the door behind her.

Langston gestures for me to sit in one of the brown leather chairs opposite his desk while he retakes his own seat.

"I must say I'm surprised that your manager finally put us in touch," Langston says. "It seemed like she was really trying to give me the run around."

"What gave you that impression?"

"She refused for weeks to tell you about my interest in speaking with you."

"Morgan always has my best interests at heart. It's her job to be in between me and everyone who wants to get to me. She knows when to filter unimportant things out and when to bring the others to me. So I guess you should feel lucky you finally made the cut."

The harsh tone of my words is purposeful. Not because I want him to believe I'm an asshole but because I need him to know that I am not the naive teenager I once was. The one who was so excited and starry eyed to have an opportunity that I took the first one that was presented to me. The opportunity that was toxic and exploitative and gave me all that I dreamed of, but at a price so high I nearly lost myself. That naive 19 year old boy was chewed up and spit out and what is left is a 29 year old man who won't make the same mistakes of the past.

Langston's jaw clenches at my words but he quickly covers his annoyance with a smirk.

"So let's not waste any more time and get right to the chase. I've followed you since the beginning of your career and you're extremely talented, which is why I want you to join us here at Silver Spoon."

Langston leans forward placing his elbows on his desk and interlocks his fingers before he continues speaking.

"I know why you didn't resign with that other label and I want to do things differently."

I raise my eyebrows in surprise at his statement because I never publicly said why I didn't renew my contract, instead deciding to separate as amicably as possible by not airing out all of my grievances and frustrations.

"Really?" I say slowly. "And why is that?"

"Because they were holding you back from your full potential."

Langston speaks as if he knows me, as if less than an hour ago I wouldn't have walked past him on the street without a single clue who he was. To him, he's saying all the right things about wanting to make me more successful and more famous but in reality it's all wrong.

"You have the raw talent of someone that should be the face of the industry. Billboards, commercials, tours, you name it, it can all be yours. Women love your voice and persona. You're still in good shape. We can play up the sex appeal and they won't be able to get enough of you."

Langston continues on, outlining his plan for me with his label, pitching me all the ways I can be more successful and have more money and more opportunities.

More. More. More.

"But what if that isn't what I want?," I ask, cutting him off. "The fame and the fortune and the women. What if I want to do something different?"

I pose the question as a hypothetical, but it's more accurate than anything Langston has said this entire meeting. I don't want to be the Sonny that I was before, placed in the box and forced to portray myself in the way the label thought would benefit themselves the most regardless of what *I* wanted.

"Of course you want it," he says chuckling. "You made it. You got yourself and your family out the hood which was always the goal, right? You've done well but it's time to aim higher, bigger. It's what everyone wants and with my help you can have it."

And there it is.

Men like Langston think that they know best and prey on young aspiring artists claiming that they can give them the world and everything they've ever dreamed of. But in reality they just want to serve their own best interests and everything else is secondary.

"Listen Langston," I say. "I appreciate the interest, but this isn't going to work between us."

His surprise from my words is evident by the expression on his face. I stand from my seat, done with the conversation. My hand is on the doorknob poised to leave this room when Langston's voice stops me.

"What would your father want of you?"

I pause and turn back to him "The fuck did you say?"

He's standing, facing me while he leans back against his desk with his arms crossed over his chest.

"From what I hear you were close with your father, and it was truly tragic how you lost him."

Langston pauses to give what is supposed to be a sympathetic smile and nod.

"He wouldn't want his only son to do something so stupid as to walk away from a deal as good as this one would he?"

I wiggle my fingers and take a deep breath using every last shred of my willpower to stop myself from punching him straight in the nose for having the audacity to bring up my father.

Langston must take my pause as contemplation because he continues speaking, unaware of the rage coursing through me.

"Sonny, be smart about this. You've been on hiatus for years now, offers aren't going to keep coming in. This is the best deal you're going to receive and if you walk out that door, it's off the table."

"You really think you have me all figured out huh," I scoff. "But see if I really needed you, you wouldn't have been begging my manager to even have the ability to have a meeting with me. I don't need a partnership with a lowlife like you who just wants to exploit me.”

I yank the door open but stop and turn back to Langston. " Oh, and since you know my father so well, you should thank him for being the only reason you aren't laid out on the floor right now. He taught me to pick my battles and you're not worth the fight.”

I walk out the door and don't even say a word to Xavier. He just follows my lead walking a few steps behind me as we walk back to the car.

My phone buzzes in my pocket and when I pull it out and look at it I see it's a message from Morgan asking for an update on the meeting when it's finished. I start to type out an angry message telling her that I knew this meeting would be a waste of time. I hit backspace and delete it all in favor of echoing Morgan's words from a few days ago back to her.

me

You can't keep doing the same things and expect a different outcome.

18
Laila

My favorite part about my job is photography. The social media aspect of it goes hand in hand with it, but something about capturing the beauty of our products makes me so happy.

When Cass first brought up the idea of doing a photoshoot with Bryce my gut reaction was against it. Then he agreed to it, and I thought about it more and my brain immediately started to put the pieces together for how I wanted it to look. Diffused light to create softness, a grainy texture added during editing, overall less posed and more relaxed.

We haven't officially moved into our new *Lovely Day* location yet, opting to finish packing up the last of the preorders from our launch before transitioning here. That decision makes choosing to do the photoshoot with Bryce at the new location even more appealing to me. It's bare bones, an empty canvas of brick walls and hardwood floors and huge windows that allow the best light. And my nosey friends won't be hovering around making it awkward.

"You're too stiff," I say, pulling the camera down from my eye.

We've been shooting for a decent amount of time and I probably only have a handful of pictures that have turned out okay.

"I'm just sitting here."

I chew on my bottom lip and turn my head to the side trying to figure out where I can make an adjustment. The pieces themselves are all there. Bryce looks good, too good, in a casual outfit of jeans and a collared shirt. He's sitting on a stool, some of our products are arranged on a stool next to him. The background looks exactly how I wanted. It's a bright sunny day and even some of the windows are open since the weather is finally starting to warm up and there's a nice breeze.

I step forward and fix the collar on his shirt and rest my hands on his shoulders, pushing my fingers into the muscles.

"Your shoulders are tense."

"I'm just sitting here," he replies.

I push harder until I feel the strained muscles soften as he relaxes.

"Yeah, but you're sitting like someone's forcing you to, not like you're actually having a good time."

"Here, let me show you," I say, pulling on his hand to get him to stand from the stool.

Bryce stands and I hand him my camera and take a seat on the stool. I bring my shoulders up to my ears and look deadpan towards him, mimicking the pose that Bryce was just doing.

"It wasn't that bad," he says, laughing.

"It wasn't much better!" I say. "But here let me show you."

I show him a bunch of different posing options, easily shifting in between them to show him that it was less about being 'posed' and more about being relaxed and comfortable in front of the camera. In a lot of the shots I didn't even want him to smile

"And sometimes you don't have to look right at the camera, you can look off to the side and give different angles. It doesn't always have to look like you're getting your picture taken for the school yearbook…"

The flash of light startles me and I turn my head back to Bryce to see him taking pictures of me with my camera.

"Am I supposed to frown like you are right now?"

I scowl at him and he takes more pictures moving around to different positions imitating a photographer until I can't contain the laughter from falling from my lips. "I didn't know grumpy was the vibe you were going for, but I think you nailed it."

I stand from the stool and hold my hand out for my camera. When he hands it back, I shove him slightly. "Oh shut up."

Bryce takes his spot back on the stool and grabs my hand as I start to walk away, stopping me.

"And for the record," Bryce says, his eyes going down to my lips before slowly coming back up to my eyes. "I am having a good time."

The second half of the session goes much better than the first. Bryce's calm easy going personality is on full display, and the awkward stiffness that was so apparent on camera before is gone.

We change set ups a couple of times, getting various different shots until I'm satisfied with the number of photos.

"I think that's a wrap," I say.

It doesn't take long to pack up the few things we brought here and we walk out together.

"Do you have plans this weekend?" Bryce asks after I lock the door and we walk the short distance to his car.

"Not really. Why do you ask?"

"My mom is hosting a party for her birthday this year and she asked me to invite you."

He says it casually but that doesn't stop the immediate thumping of my chest.

"Me?" I ask. "Why?"

"She knows you came to the hospital with me, and that that wouldn't have happened if you weren't important to me," he says. "And she's my mom so she's just a little bit nosey."

I snort at that comment but then his previous words hit me. "I'm important to you?"

Bryce leans his face impossibly close to mine until we're sharing breaths. His calm and steady and mine erratic, matching the sporadic thump of my heartbeat from his closeness. He pauses, giving me space to back away, to deny him, but I don't.

The warm pressure of his lips is intoxicatingly blissful. It is gentle yet firm, conveying his passion and care all while reminding me that I am safe with him. All of me.

I'm not sure how long we're kissing for, a few seconds, a few minutes, or more, I have no idea. I'm completely lost in the orbit of us, at this moment.

I feel the absence of him when he pulls away the coolness of the air whipping through the buildings.

"Important is only the tip of the iceberg, pretty girl. When you're ready there'll be so many more words to add to that list, but for now we can go at your pace."

19
Laila

THE SOUND OF THE doorbell echoes through the house after Bryce presses the button. I shift from foot to foot, trying to calm my nerves.

"Don't be nervous," Bryce says with a soft squeeze to the hand that he holds in his. "Just be you and know that I got you."

Before I can respond the door to the house is flung open by his sister.

"Thank the lord it's you," Bryce's sister says. "Your mother is driving me crazy."

Bryce chuckles as we step inside. "You know how she is. She wants everything to be perfect."

"Which is why she should've hired a company to take care of all of this instead of putting us all to work."

"I offer to pay for it every time she throws her birthday party and every year she says that she doesn't want it."

"I know," Lauryn says, rolling her eyes. "She's stubborn as hell."

Lauryn pulls Bryce into a hug and then turns and pulls me into a hug too. I'm stunned at first by the action, because I don't come from a family of huggers, but then I wrap my arms around her and hug her back.

"I'm so happy to finally be able to actually meet you," Lauryn says.

"Me too," I reply with a smile.

"C'mon, she's in the kitchen," Lauryn says, leading the way.

"Ma, this is Laila," Bryce says, introducing us when we reach the kitchen. "Laila, this is my mom, Janet."

"Hi Laila, it's nice to meet you," she says.

"Thank you, and happy birthday. I brought these for you."

I hand her the flowers that I spent a ridiculous amount of time choosing at the florist this morning. I ultimately decided on pink lilies and red roses, something classic.

"Honey, these are beautiful, thank you. The two of you go on and wash your hands so we can finish setting up since folks are starting to arrive."

We do as she asked and wash our hands in the nearby half bathroom.

"See I told you everything is gonna be fine," Bryce says, placing a kiss on the top of my head before walking out of the bathroom.

He did the action so casually and effortlessly, as if it was no big deal. As if it didn't cause my heart to stutter and my breaths to rapidly increase.

I take another moment to myself before rejoining everyone in the kitchen. Bryce's other sister Shannon is seated at the island typing away furiously at her phone. She doesn't look up to acknowledge me and I opt not to engage and instead focus on the task given to me, to cut up the fruit.

"Bryce, go bring these pans out to your uncle on the grill."

"Yes ma'am," Bryce says, picking up the pans.

"Ms. Janet, we didn't see those tablecloths that you were looking for," a middle aged man says walking into the kitchen.

Bryce's mom sighs and shakes her head. "I know they're in there. Let me go look and see."

The kitchen is quiet except for the sounds of music playing outside in the backyard and the chopping sounds of Lauryn and I doing the things we were tasked with by her mom.

"Soooo," Lauryn says next to me when she finishes the salad she was tasked with making. "What's going on with you and my brother?"

I shake my head. "I'm not sure what you mean."

"I mean I was just wondering if you and B are together or..."

Lauryn lets the end of her sentence hang, waiting for my answer.

I knew it was a possibility someone would ask me about my relationship with Bryce, but I still feel unprepared to answer. I look out the windows that overlook the backyard and see Bryce talking and laughing with a small group of people who have just arrived.

"Um, not really," I reply. "We're just good friends."

"Interesting," Lauryn says.

"That's not really how it works," Shannon says looking up from her phone.

"Excuse me?"

"You said 'not really' but that's not an answer. You either are or you aren't."

I pause mid cut at her words. The tone of which doesn't sit right with me.

"It is an answer because it's the one I gave," I say calmly, my eyes locked with Shannon's. "Bryce and I *are* friends. If we ever become more than that, he can tell you himself if he wants to."

Shannon snorts and rolls her eyes, murmuring something I can't hear under her breath. Lauryn shoots her a look and Shannon stares back, the two of them locked in a silent conversation.

"Am I missing something?" I ask, holding back the less nice version of the question that was on the tip of my tongue.

Lauryn breaks eye contact first and smiles at me. "Well no, it's just that B hasn't ever brought 'just a friend' home before. So we were just surprised, that's all. And you call him Bryce, he usually only goes by Sonny. "

"Oh, well I guess there's a first time for everything," I say with a shrug, trying not to read too deeply into Lauryn's words.

"Leave it to a man to not be able to see what's right in front of him," Bryce's mom says, walking back into the room with the tablecloths in her hand.

Bryce's mom must notice the energy in the room as she looks between the three of us. "Everything alright in here?"

I nod my head, "Yes ma'am."

"I'm going to go check on RJ," Shannon says, sliding off her chair.

Lauryn nudges me. "Don't pay her any mind."

Without Shannon, the mood in the kitchen improves dramatically. Talking with Lauryn and Bryce's mom comes easily as we finish preparing for the party. They don't interrogate me, or make me feel uncomfortable, like my nerves made me want to believe before I arrived. If anything it's the opposite. Before I know it, everything that was left to do is finished.

"Is there anything else you need help with?"

"You've done more than enough. I've got it from here."

"Are you sure?" I ask. "I don't mind."

"Honey, go on and find that son of mine and enjoy yourself," she replies, shooing me out of the kitchen.

Someone walks in and gets her attention, whisking her away to do something else, so I follow her direction and go off in search of Bryce.

In the backyard, I see that the party is in full swing. The music has been turned up and there are a lot of people talking, eating and overall enjoying themselves. I scan the yard for Bryce and see him across the yard with who I assume to be his uncle on the grill. I leave him to talk and grab a seltzer from a nearby cooler and take a seat at an empty table.

Only a few minutes pass before I see Bryce walking towards me.

"Hey you good?" he asks.

"Yeah, I'm fine."

"You sure? You're over here hiding out by yourself," he says, skeptical.

"I'm not hiding," I argue back. "I was just hanging back and letting you be with your family."

"Nah, none of that. Let's go get you a plate."

He takes my hand and leads us to where all the food is set out on warmers and we take our spot at the end of the line.

"Is this all your family?" I ask, looking around at the growing number of people arriving.

"For the most part yeah. There's some of my mom's friends, but she's been friends with them for forever so they're damn near family at this point. Everyone else is related to me in one way or another."

He points out different people throughout the yard, aunts, uncles and cousins, telling me their names.

"Wow," I reply. "I didn't realize people actually had big family gatherings like this."

"You don't have family parties?"

"Not like this," I say, gesturing to all the people. "My mom is an only child and she isn't close with her extended family."

"My mom is one of six and my dad was one of four and they all had a bunch of kids so I'm used to having a lot of family around for events and stuff."

We inch forward in the line and the older man Bryce was talking to earlier, walks up to the both of us. "This you nephew?"

He holds his hand out to me and I take it, shaking it. "Hi, I'm Laila."

"Laila, what is a beautiful lady like yourself doing with a knucklehead like this one here?"

"You trying to take my girl right in front of me Unc?" Bryce says, joking. "That's cold blooded."

"Just calling it like I see it nephew," Bryce's uncle says before turning back to me. "If Bryce here ever gives you any trouble, you let me know and I'll make sure to get him in line."

I laugh at the back and forth that Bryce and his uncle go through before his uncle pats him on the shoulder and leaves.

"That's Uncle Henry, my mom's brother. He's a smooth talker but he's harmless."

Bryce and I finally make it to the front of the line and make our plates of food. It's a full barbecue spread and everything looks delicious, so I fill my plate up with a little bit of everything. Bryce leads us to a table full of people around our age and he introduces me to his cousins. We eat and talk and I find myself able to completely relax as the night goes on.

20
Sonny

"Run that back again."

Blue presses a button and the song starts to play through the headphones again. I close my eyes and listen intently. I listen, trying to find any flaws or things I want to change but when the song ends, I come up empty. I know that Blue will tweak a few things to clean it up before it's really finished, but I'm really happy with it.

I open my eyes and pull the headphones down from my ears as the final notes of the song play, relishing in the feeling of finishing another song.

There's something incredible about when what starts out as just a few lines in my head turns into a whole song playing through the speakers. It's been a decade of making music professionally and still this feeling hits me every time I make a song I connect deeply with.

I hang my headphones on the mic and step out of the booth. I take a seat in the chair next to Blue.

"Nigga that was magic," Blue says. "I knew that beat would be perfect for you."

Blue had sent me a couple of beats earlier in the week to see if I was interested in any of them. They all matched the vibe, but this one in particular called out to me.

"Yeah it flowed really easy, I haven't written a song in the booth in a long time and definitely not something that I like this much."

"Your heart wasn't in that other shit and it shows. Don't get me wrong it was a hit and your vocals carried it but this," Blue points to his monitor that has the song we just made. "This is too good to stay in the drafts. You're on your lover boy shit and this is where you belonged all along."

"Lover boy shit," I echo, laughing.

"So what's the plan, are you back or what?"

I run a hand over my hair and sigh. "Man, I wish I had the answer. I had a meeting with a label a few weeks ago and it just reminded me how much I don't want to be in that environment again. It's toxic."

"So then don't."

I shake my head. "It's not that easy. I took time off to figure shit out and I still found myself writing songs. I don't think I'm ready to give it up yet."

"Nah, I didn't mean give up music," Blue says. "I mean do it on your own. Then no one can tell you what you can and can't do."

"You forreal?"

"Shit, why not?"

"Because it could all go really fucking wrong and then its all on me."

"Or it could all go right," Blue says, shrugging. "It could be your key to greatness. You can't be so afraid of things going wrong, cause that's always a possibility. If you let it hold you back you'll never know."

Blue stands from his chair. "I'ma step out for a minute for a smoke and call my lady."

"For sure, do your thing," I reply.

You can't keep doing the same things and expect a different outcome.

Morgan's words hit me again.

Being an independent artist was never something that I ever considered. I always thought that I would be signed to a label, it was just a given. Now, for the first time, I give myself permission to dream outside of the confines that I placed on myself.

21
Laila

TODAY WAS ANOTHER DAY of working later than I intended because I was so wrapped up in my work I didn't realize the time. I worked on editing the pictures from my photoshoot with Bryce and trying to get started on putting all of the pieces of the campaign together. I sent over a few of my favorite pictures to him while I was editing and he loved them, responding with a bunch of fire emojis and truly hyping me up more than himself even though he was the focus of the photo.

Of course I also forgot to eat, but instead of eating alone, I decided to order Jamaican food for Zara and I to eat in between her clients. I pick up the food from the restaurant and the walk to the shop that Zara works at, which is only a couple of streets over.

Marcus, the owner of the shop, is lining someone up in his chair when I step through the front door. He gives me a silent hello with a head nod and I give him one of my own before walking back towards Zara's area. None of the other barbers acknowledge me as I make my way to the back. Some of them glance in my direction, but they quickly avert their eyes back to their clients without a word.

Zara is walking out of the laundry area, rolling a laundry cart full of towels when she sees me with the bags of food.

"Ahhh, you're the best. Let me put these away really quick and I'll meet you in the break room."

"Okay."

The break room is a small room with an old fridge that makes a bunch of noises and a small table with mismatched chairs. I set the bags on the table and pull out the cartons of food. My stomach growls as I pull each thing out, jerk chicken, rice and peas, cabbage and yams. All of it smells delicious and I can't help but dive in.

Five minutes later Zara comes and joins me.

"I am so tired of cleaning up after these grown ass men," Zara says, plopping down in the seat next to me.

"Is it still that bad?"

"Niggas act like they're allergic to cleaning up and doing laundry but what else is new." Zara rolls her eyes. "I walked into the shop this morning and there were two clean towels. What the hell are we supposed to do with that?"

I shake my head in disbelief. "Is Marcus doing anything about it?"

For the past few months Zara has told me about how frustrated she's been with her job. Nothing to do with her clients, or her actual work, but everything else that comes along with working with other people. Lack of cleaning up after themselves and simply being inconsiderate were at the top of her list of annoyances.

"He says he's talked to the guys, but nothing's changed, so the 'talking' isn't doing a damn thing."

"Have you put any more thought into leaving?" I ask, my voice low to avoid anyone overhearing.

"Yeah, but there aren't a ton of options. I love working in Rosewood, but most of the other shops don't have any open chairs, or if they do the vibes are terrible."

Zara is arguably the best barber in Rosewood and the people who would argue against me are probably misogynistic who don't think a woman can do the job as well as a man. Her books are usually filled up weeks in advance and all of her clients are loyal and rave about her all over social media.

"Yeah, well we gotta keep looking cause the vibes here aren't it either."

"Ain't that the truth," she says.

I haven't seen Zara much this past weekend so as we eat, we fill each other in on everything that's new. For her it's a new guy that's been added to her roster. She went to an art gallery exhibition and hooked up with one of the artists. For me, it leaves me talking about Bryce. I tell her about my time at his mom's birthday party last week.

"I had a really good time," I say, finishing the story. "Being around his family was nice."

"Meeting the family," Zara says, raising her eyebrows. "Interesting."

"What?"

"That's not casual shit."

"It doesn't have to mean anything."

"Just because it doesn't have to mean anything, doesn't mean that it doesn't mean anything," Zara says. "Did he introduce you to everyone as his friend?"

"Well no, he introduced me as Laila and ..."

I pause knowing my next words would just prove Zara's point.

"And?"

"There was a time when he was talking to his uncle and he called me 'his girl' but -"

"Aht, keep your excuses," Zara interrupts. "That's all I needed to know."

"We're just friends," I argue.

"Girl, just because you're being delusional doesn't mean that I'm going to be. That man would gladly knock those cobwebs off for you the second you ask."

I gasp and toss my napkin at her and then we both fall into a fit of giggles.

After we collect ourselves, Zara turns serious again.

"No but seriously, why are you so afraid of going there with him?"

I should've known that Zara wouldn't hold back from asking me the hard things, but still my breath catches in my throat at the question. The question that I haven't let myself think about because it has felt too raw to face those emotions head on instead of avoiding them, like I have since Bryce told me that he was interested in me.

I let out a deep breath. "Does it feel like it's moving too fast to you?"

"Fast? You've had that man in the friend zone for forever. It's not been fast."

"No, not like that," I say. "I mean fast since I ended things with Devin."

Zara smacks her teeth. "Girl, you could have gone out with another guy the next day after you found out his triflin' ass was cheating on you and you wouldn't have heard a peep from me. There's no timeline for what's 'right'. But only you can really answer whether or not it's too soon, because it's your life not mine."

"I know I know," I say. "But after Devin I feel like I can't trust myself anymore. He had a whole baby and I didn't know."

"Don't do that."

"Do what?" I ask, raising an eyebrow.

"Leave out the part where your gut was right. You knew he wasn't being truthful to you, but he gaslit you into believing that you were the one in the wrong, when in reality it was all him. Do not let that toxic boy get in the way of you finding your person."

Zara reaches out and holds my hand. "You didn't know it was a baby, but you knew it was something so you can't deny your intuition."

"It's just so damn easy with Bryce and I feel like I'm missing something. I keep waiting for the other shoe to drop and it hasn't."

"Stop holding your breath for something that may never come when you could be out enjoying your life. Life is too damn short to not take the risk sometimes."

"You're right," I reply. "Though that same logic could've been applied for that time I wanted bangs, but you drew the line at that."

One night after my breakup, I had been crying on the couch with a bowl of ice cream. I was so tired of being sad and decided that I wanted a change and to do something impulsive. Bangs seemed like an excellent choice. I was convinced that bangs would fix my problems and make me feel better. I asked Zara to cut them for me and she flat out refused. She said that she loved me too much to give me 'breakup bangs'.

Zara was adamant that it was a bad choice. I eventually was able to get her to compromise to cutting them for me if I still wanted them in a week's time.

Within a week I had pulled myself together, and even though I was still sad, I wasn't the sad girl crying on the couch desperately seeking some form of control in her life.

"Hell yeah!" Zara says. "You never once said that you wanted bangs before that night. You were doing the bare minimum to survive at that time. There was no chance you were going to put in the effort to style them and be happy with them. After the newness wore off you would've been crying to me about how much you hated them."

"You're right I definitely would have," I say, laughing.

"Yo Zara, you have a client," someone calls out.

Zara looks down at her watch. "He must be early. You know as soon as the weather gets a little warm, everybody needs a fresh cut."

We stand and gather the trash from our food, tossing it all into the trash can by the fridge. We walk together to the door of the break room and Zara stops in her tracks at the threshold and frowns.

A man is standing at her station talking on the phone. His back is to us but I can see his face in the mirror at Zara's station. He's tall, at least 6'6" and his skin a deep mahogany hue.

Zara's body language tells me that she's familiar with him, but he wasn't who she was expecting to see. He sees Zara and I in the reflection in the mirror and locks eyes with her. They stare each other down all while he continues his conversation on the phone.

"Who's that," I whisper.

Zara turns to me, rolls her eyes and speaks loudly. "A pain in my ass. I'll tell you about it later."

She pulls me into a quick hug goodbye before walking over to the mystery man.

22
Laila

I shut my laptop and stand from my desk, walking quickly to the back door of our office. I open the door and standing there with a beautiful bouquet of pink roses is Bryce. I can't stop the grin that instantly comes to my face.

"Wow these are beautiful," I say, taking the flowers from him.

I step back to let him step inside the building and we walk together back to my desk. I set the flowers down next to my laptop.

"You didn't think I forgot did you?"

Like clockwork, as my previous flowers started to brown and wilt, the delivery man would arrive with new ones to replace them. Every. Single. Time. Since the first time he bought me flowers.

"No," I say. "We've just both been very busy and we haven't seen each other in a minute, so I would have understood if you were too busy."

"You know you don't have to do that right?"

"Do what?"

Bryce takes my hand and rubs the back of my hand with his thumb. "Lower your expectations of other people."

"Easier said than done," I reply. "Sometimes giving other people the power to let you down leaves you as the one with hurt feelings."

Bryce cocks his head to the side and looks at me intensely. I can tell he wants me to elaborate on the little piece of my trauma that I just shared. Before he can respond, I change the subject. "I thought you were going to be in the studio all day today."

"I am, we made a lot of progress today cleaning things up and putting finishing touches on the album. I just needed a little bit of a break. Also like you said, I haven't seen you in a minute so I thought I'd bring you your flowers before I head back."

"Thank you," I say. "Does that finally mean I can get a little sneak peek?"

Bryce has spent hours and hours in the studio working on the album, but he's kept it very close to his chest and hasn't shared any of it with me.

"Maybe," he says, an amused look on his face.

I take it as a victory because everything before this has been a hard no. He hasn't wanted to share anything about the project yet, the whole thing just between him and Blue.

"What you got going on today?" Bryce asks.

"Actually," I say, grabbing my laptop. "I just finished editing some of the spreads from our photoshoot and was going to send them over to Morgan for approval."

I flip the computer around to show Bryce the things I've been working on. He scrolls through the photos and graphics.

"Damn, you really did your thing with this photoshoot. This is amazing."

"Thank you," I say, smiling. "If Morgan doesn't have any notes we plan to release this next week right with our summer restock."

"Are you busy tomorrow night?

I shake my head.

"Good, I have a surprise for you. I'll have a driver come and pick you up at 7."

"Are you asking me on a date?"

"If I say 'yes' is it going to scare you off?"

I bite my bottom lip, those flutters that plagued my body when Bryce and I first decided to be friends, back again. I don't trust myself to speak so I just shake my head.

"Good, because I am asking you to go on a date with me. Don't overthink it," Bryce says, his dark brown eyes staring into mine. "I'll see you tomorrow, okay?"

I nod. "See you tomorrow."

Bryce brings my hand up to his lips and kisses my knuckles. I watch him walk away, leaving through the back door just like he came.

***

Bryce refused to tell me where we we're going for our date. I texted him while I was choosing my outfit, fishing for any details he would give me. He didn't reveal anything, simply telling me that whatever I chose would be perfect.

I opt for a black satin wrap midi dress, that hugs my body in all the places I want it to, with a slit on one side that shows just the right amount of leg. I pair it with a simple pair of heels.

The click of my heels echo as I walk through the lobby of my building. A blacked out SUV is parked right outside the doors, a man in a dark gray suit standing on the passenger side.

I step out the door and make eye contact with the man.

"Ms. Eden?" the man asks.

I nod and he steps aside, opening the back door for me to get in. Once I've slid into the seat, he closes the door and walks around to get into the driver's seat. He puts the car in drive and starts on the way to our destination.

I sit back in my seat and watch the buildings pass by as we leave Rosewood, heading towards Chicago. My phone chimes and I pick it up, seeing it's a message from Zara.

She wasn't home yet when I was getting ready, still at the shop with a late night client. I sent her a picture of me in my outfit on my way out to get her opinion. I open her message and giggle at the fire and heart eye emojis that she sent in response.

I am so wrapped up in texting Zara, I don't notice when the car stops until the driver says something.

"We've arrived, Ms. Eden."

My head snaps up and I look around, trying to find my bearings and figure out where I am. I'm confused, seeing only the water of the lake until my eyes land on the ferris wheel.

The Pier.

I haven't been here in years, probably since middle school for a field trip. Parked next to us is an identical blacked out SUV and I watch as Bryce steps out from the backseat.

Bryce always looks good, but something about the calm confidence of his demeanor as he strides past the front of the car dressed up just for me has me clenching my thighs together as I wait. He pulls my door open and flashes me a smile, both of the dimples in his cheeks on display.

He offers me his hand to help me out of the car. As I stand next to him, he does a slow perusal of my body, starting at my feet and working his way up until we lock eyes.

"Perfect. Just like I said," he murmurs.

Warmth spreads through my body at his words. Bryce takes my hand in his and starts to lead me away from the trucks. I scan our surroundings, searching for the crowds of people I know are usually always abundant especially during the summer.

"You don't have to worry about that," Bryce says, acknowledging the fears I hadn't voiced aloud.

I scrunch my face in confusion. "What do you mean?"

"You made it clear that you want this," he motions between the two of us. "To be private. I wouldn't ask you on a date just to violate that."

My shoulders, that I hadn't realized were raised, relax. I allow myself to let go of the lingering tension in my body. Bryce takes my hand in his, interlacing our fingers as he leads me to our destination.

We walk past the row of boats lined up at the dock until we reach the one at the very end, the largest of them all.

My eyes widen at the yacht in front of us. "All of this is for us?"

"Of course."

The sun is just starting to set as we step on the boat. One of the members of the staff greets us telling us to enjoy ourselves and that dinner would be ready soon. Bryce leads me up to the top deck.

The sky is a beautiful combination of yellows and pinks, the sun passing behind the buildings. I smile at the beauty of it all. With no other boats around it feels like we're in our own little haven.

My eyes land on one of the many pots of flowers around the deck, reminding me of something that had been on my mind for a while.

"Why do you always send me flowers?"

"When I first looked at your Instagram you had a bunch of pictures with you and your friends but two of your highlights were sunsets and flowers. I can't give you sunsets, that's all straight from the man upstairs, but I can give you flowers."

"Oh," I say softly, taken aback by the deep meaning behind his actions.

The boat is moving, pushing further away from dock and out onto the lake. I watch as the buildings retreat, getting further and further away when Bryce speaks again.

"Why do I make you nervous?"

"Who says that you do?" I ask.

"You do," Bryce replies. "Everytime you realize that you've let me in, you shut down again."

I take in deep breaths of the fresh air, preparing myself to tell a story that I've never had to tell in its entirety to another person.

"A few months before we ran into each other again, I got out of a really bad relationship," I pause, needing a minute before continuing.

I feel Bryce come up behind me, his front to my back and his hands placed on the railing right next to mine. It's an action that would feel constricting with anyone else, but it's comforting from him.

"He was my first serious relationship. I had dated some before, but nothing significant or long term. Things moved fast but he seemed to be everything that I wanted. He said and did all the right things until he just didn't. It felt like he changed overnight."

"He put his hands on you?" Bryce asks, his voice low.

I shake my head. "No, nothing physical. He started lying. It was little things at first and then it turned into him lying about his whereabouts and hiding his phone. When I would bring it up he would always talk himself out of it, tell me that I was crazy or looking for things to be wrong."

I let out a humorless chuckle. "Until he couldn't use that excuse anymore, because he had gotten another woman pregnant."

Bryce lets out a breath. "Shit."

"That's when I finally woke up and stopped being so oblivious to his bullshit. But the damage was already done."

"You can't blame yourself for the actions of someone else, Laila."

"No, but I can blame myself for my own actions. I should have seen what was happening for what it was."

"You *should* give yourself grace. You didn't deserve what you experienced and you shouldn't minimize the trauma of the experience."

"That's hard to do when it's the reason letting you in feels so damn daunting."

We both stand in silence for a moment, the last remnants of light giving away to the night sky.

"My pops used to tell me all the time that the only thing worse than failure is regret," Bryce turns me around to face him. "I don't want to regret not trying with you. I care about you and I will always do everything in my power to show you that. I will never treat you roughly, because hurting you isn't an option."

We've stepped out of the pretense of 'just friends' that I put us in before and fallen into something much more. The fear and anxiety that I would have expected to come with that realization is notably absent.

"You said we're going at my pace, right?" I ask.

My heels bring us closer to eye to eye, but I still have to tip my head slightly.

The look in his eyes is full of sincerity, the feeling knocking on the carefully guarded walls I've built around my heart. My eyes drop to admire his full lips before I flick my eyes back up to his heated gaze.

He dips his head in agreement. "Following your lead."

I don't let myself think as I close the miniscule distance between us until our lips meet. This kiss isn't gentle or soft like our last, instead it's forceful and assertive, both of us finally allowing ourselves to indulge in the heat that's been simmering between us. Months of attraction erupting into a fiery blaze.

Bryce's tongue presses to my lips and I immediately surrender, opening for him to explore my mouth with his. I sink my teeth into his bottom lip, biting before soothing the pain away with a few swipes of my tongue.

One of his hands cups my cheek while the other travels down to grip my ass. He squeezes and pulls me closer to him, the hard length of him pressing into my stomach as our lips continue to tangle. His lips move down the curve of my neck, nipping at my skin causing a moan to slip through my lips.

I slide my hand between us, running my hand up and down the length of him through his pants and squeezing.

"Don't do that," Bryce growls into my neck.

I pull back slightly to look him in the eye and arch a brow. "Why not?"

"Because if we go down that path, it's gonna end with you getting fucked bent over this railing."

I hum, the seat of my panties getting wet at his words.

I should listen and put an end to this, for so many reasons, including the fact we're out in the open and the staff of the boat isn't that far away.

But I don't want to.

I don't want to keep holding him at arm's length like I have been for the past few moments. I don't want to keep denying the feelings that have between us despite my attempts to shield myself and lock away my heart.

I don't want to be afraid anymore.

"Maybe that's my goal."

He shakes his head. "You're fucking trouble."

Bryce's hand slides up my exposed leg, maneuvering under the fabric of my dress to the apex of my thighs. The pad of his thumb grazes over my clit and I shiver from the touch.

He nudges my panties to the side, running a finger through the wetness of my slit while his thumb works in slow, firm circles on my clit. Bryce's lips meet mine again for slow unhurried kisses that cause my nipples to strain against the fabric of my dress.

"Fuck," I pant.

His thick finger glides in and out of me and I rock into the base of his hand inching closer and closer to ecstasy. I'm so close to coming undone that I can barely catch my breath.

"Give it to me, baby."

Another of Bryce's fingers joins the first and he curls them in a motion that is exactly what I need to send me over the edge. My orgasm rushes over me in one big wave sending tingles of pleasure through my body.

Bryce pulls his fingers from my core, bringing them to his mouth. His eyes are locked on mine as he sucks each finger clean. The action sends a shiver down my spine, the desire that lies low in my belly for him intensifying.

He flips me around and presses my front to the guard rail of the boat and I can feel just how much he wants me.

"I don't have a condom," he murmurs.

"I'm on birth control."

Bryce places kisses down my neck eliciting another moan from me.

"If you don't want this I need you to tell me now," he says, his lips close to my ear, giving me an out if I want it.

I don't.

I press my ass back into him, grinding against his hardness.

"Fuck, Laila," Bryce breathes.

He lifts my skirt and yanks my panties down. I hiss at the intrusion as he pushes into me, the shock of the intrusion quickly turning into a moan of pleasure. He strokes me slowly at first, giving me time to adjust before his pace quickens.

"Is this what you wanted?" Bryce asks, pulling nearly all the way out before plunging himself deep into me again. "For me to be fucking this pretty pussy."

I can't answer, unable to form a coherent thought as he continues stroking me, the feel of his dick causing my pussy to clench.

I feel his hand come to my hair, taking a handful and tugging my head back.

"I asked if this is what you wanted," Bryce says, his voice rough.

"Yes," I gasp.

"Good girl."

This orgasm comes without warning, rippling through me and causing my body to jerk. Bryce follows soon after, spilling into me with a groan.

I brace myself against the railing catching my breath while Bryce adjusts himself back into his pants.

Bryce places a soft kiss to my shoulder before he reaches down to pull my panties the rest of the way down my legs, helping me step out of them. He bends down and picks them up, sliding them into his pants pocket.

"You won't be needing those anymore," he says. "Let's go get you cleaned up before dinner."

23
Laila

THE MOMENTS LEADING UP to interacting with my mother always leave me feeling like there's a weight attached directly to my chest. A heavy, try to clear your throat but it doesn't ease the pressure, kind of weight. The kind that I have to decompress from after the interaction is done.

I have been avoiding her calls for weeks, partially because I have so much going on in my own life, and also because I wasn't in the mood to play personal ATM for all her needs. But a few days ago she texted me saying that we should get lunch to catch up and reluctantly I agreed.

I have that heavy feeling now as I wait for her at the restaurant and wish I had never agreed in the first place. I have just decided on ordering a peach bellini when my mother arrives at the table. I stand and hug her, a quick small pat on the back that doesn't really give any affection at all.

"How are you?" I ask as we pull apart.

"I'm fine," she replies. "The parking situation here is dreadful. If I had known, I would have said for us to choose another restaurant."

"Oh I wouldn't know," I reply with a shrug. "I usually take the train, but their food is really good."

Our waitress comes to our table a few moments later, setting down a carafe of water and taking down our drink orders before darting away again to give us more time to look over the food menu.

We scan our menus quietly. I've been here a few times but I still like to look to see what new things have been added to the menu even though I always get the same thing, shrimp and grits.

Despite the growing lunch crowd, our food and drinks come out relatively quickly and it gives us something else to focus on other than the strained small talk.

"You look so much prettier when you wear your hair down instead of up like that," my mom says, flipping her own long straightened strands over her shoulder.

I had dragged my feet getting ready this morning, wishing that I hadn't agreed to brunch and could spend more time with Bryce instead. I procrastinated so much that instead of taking the time to fix my curls and make them look nice, I used a scrunchie and some gel to pull my hair up into a messy bun.

"There's nothing wrong with my hair, it's just up in a bun."

"Yes, but you should always show the best version of yourself when you're out and about, especially since you're single. You never know who you might run into."

"My whole life goal isn't to get the attention of a man," I say, rolling my eyes.

"I'm not saying that," she says with an exasperated sigh. "I'm just saying that you don't want to close yourself off."

"I'm not closed off."

She ignores my statement and continues on with more questions.

"So is there anything interesting going on with you? Are you seeing anyone? Or are you still wrapped up in that job of yours?"

I clench my jaw, trying to unhear the critique in her voice.

"I actually just started seeing someone," I say, smiling at the image in my head of Bryce in my apartment this morning.

"Is it something serious or just a fling?"

I don't know how to answer that. Unsure how to explain that despite my best efforts I was falling, no, had fallen, for a man that I promised myself I wouldn't because the act of falling terrifies me. How does one put into words that it was the fact that I felt so at ease and so comfortable quickly and that within itself was the problem.

I don't want to get that deep into my feelings for Bryce with my mom so I choose a short and simple answer.

"We're taking things slow and just seeing where they go."

My mom hums and eats a few bites of her food before she responds.

"Let's hope he's nothing like the last guy. What was his name again?"

I swallow a bite of food. "Devin."

"Yes, Devin. He sure was handsome, it's a shame you couldn't keep him."

She says this casually as if Devin was a library book that had reached its return date and not a man who lied and cheated on me for months until his lies caught up to him and he couldn't lie anymore.

I don't respond, choosing instead to down the rest of my second bellini even though it was still half full. I exhale a deep breath when I set the champagne flute down on the table.

Our waitress comes and asks us if we need anything, clearing away empty plates from our table as she does. My mom orders another mimosa and I just ask for the check. The waitress gives us a smile and tells me that she'll be right back with it.

The momentary interruption doesn't stop my mother from continuing her comments about my relationships.

"Well I pray this one goes better and you're protecting yourself," she says as she takes a sip of her mimosa. "You don't want to be left with a baby while the man gets to go off and live his life. I've been there and I can tell you that it's not fun."

I set my fork down and push my plate away from me, no longer hungry. "Why do you have to do that?"

The check and mimosa are set on our table by our waitress and she swiftly leaves, probably because of the palpable tension in the air.

"Do what?"

"You do realize that the kid that made your life *so hard* is sitting right here, right?"

She rolls her eyes and takes another sip of her drink. "Laila, you have always been so dramatic. Things were hard. I'm not going to sugarcoat it for you."

When I was growing up, things *were* hard. She isn't wrong about that. My mom got pregnant her sophomore year of college and wasn't able to finish her schooling after she gave birth. She worked multiple jobs, and we didn't have a lot of money, but it was what it was. It didn't come without her constant reminder that this wasn't the life that she wanted and that it was all because of my existence. As if I asked for any of it.

"It's not dramatic to want a mother who actually cares about her daughter," I say.

"I do care about you. You always had clothes on your back and food in your stomach. If my best wasn't good enough for you, I don't know what to tell you. I didn't realize I was such a bad mom."

That's my last straw for this meal.

I grab my wallet, hoping that the cash I have on me is enough to cover our total plus tip because I don't want to have to sit through the process of waiting to pay with my card.

I count through the bills I need and stuff them into the receipt holder. I stand and grab my purse.

"You don't get a trophy for doing the bare minimum," I say before turning on my heel and leaving.

24
Sonny

I HAD SURELY PASSED whatever socially acceptable time there was to watch someone as they slept but I don't give a damn. She looks peaceful, her beautiful face calm and relaxed as she sleeps.

Before Laila, I didn't know I could be so addicted to someone's presence. It had been like this before when we were just friends, when we hadn't crossed the line in the sand that she had drawn all those months ago. But now that she was mine? That feeling has only amplified and when she isn't around I want her to be.

I'm not sure why my body refuses to rest after staying up late going round after round, lost in Laila, but after only a couple hours I'm wide awake. The clock on my nightstand tells me that I only have about an hour until I'm supposed to get up to meet the guys to play ball. I already turned off the alarm I had set when I realized that no amount of counting sheep, or pretending to sleep, would actually help me to fall back asleep.

Laila shifts in her sleep, going from her head resting on my chest to lying on her other side facing away from me. I take this as my opportunity to get up. I know that the chances of me unintentionally waking her up continue to increase the longer I lie in the bed awake next to her. I ease out of the bed and walk out to the living room. I don't bother to turn on any lights and instead let the moonlight and my knowledge of my place guide me to my piano. It is far too late, or early depending on how you think about it, to play anything but working on lyrics felt better in front of my piano than anywhere else.

I grab my journal and my pair of over ear headphones to listen to the beats and lose myself in the words. I'm so absorbed in what I'm doing that I don't notice Laila until she's sliding onto the piano bench next to me.

I pull the headphones off and place them on the little table next to my piano.

"Hey you," Laila murmurs.

I place a small kiss on her lips. "Hey yourself. I didn't wake you did I?"

"No, I have a hair appointment in a little bit so I had an alarm set," Laila says, yawning. "What are you working on?"

"I was working through a new song and then I have a meeting with Morgan after I get back from the gym to talk about all the promo and events she thinks I should do before the release of the album."

"Ooo fun. Is there anything solidified yet?"

"We've started doing a schedule for social media posts, there's a couple interviews and she also wants me to have an album release party. We've also started planning some small events, pop ups in different cities, but for small groups to listen to some songs.

"I think those are all great ideas. You've talked about wanting to really connect with your audience and show them more of who you are and all of that will definitely help accomplish that."

I smile. "I agree, all of this has definitely been a labor of love, but I think I might actually like the result once it's all said and done."

Laila wraps her arms around my neck and places a kiss on my cheek. "I know you will."

I wrap one arm around her waist and pull her onto my lap so she's straddling me. One of Laila's hands travels down my bare chest and rests right above my heart. In my attempt to not wake her I didn't grab a shirt to put on.

"Do these have a meaning?" Laila asks, her eyes still focused on the ink.

Her fingers are lightly running over the tattoo on the left of my chest. The only ink on my body, because nothing else has made me feel strong enough to want to have it on me for forever.

Two lines of six numbers, small and simple, exactly how I wanted it.

Laila's eyes are focused on watching her finger as she traces the numbers but I still look at her as I respond.

"They're dates that had a significant impact on me. The first one is April 17, 2019. The day my dad died."

Laila's fingers stop moving and she snaps her head up to look at me.

"I'm sorry, I didn't know."

I shake my head. "There's nothing to apologize for."

"And the other one is -"

"October 22, 2020," Laila interjects.

I nod. I can see the wheels turning as she processes the date, trying to figure out why it's there with the other one.

"The day I met you."

At my words she goes still, staring at the tattoo until her eyes flick up to mine.

"What? What do you mean? When did you get these?"

The words tumble out of her mouth, one after the other.

"A couple months after my tour ended. I wasn't in a great place mentally. I felt like I was almost in mourning after everything that had happened. But I couldn't get the girl that reminded me that I wasn't the arrogant asshole I was allowing myself to become, out of my head. She gave me the push to start living for me and I wanted to always remember that day."

"I-I don't know what to say," she says.

I take her fingers and bring them up to my lips, pressing a soft kiss to them. "You don't have to. I'm all in with you, and this tattoo now has even deeper meaning for me because of it."

"But this just started. How can you be so sure?"

I hear the fear in her voice.

The doubt.

The hesitance.

I reach into the pocket of my basketball shorts to get my phone. I'm not sure if it'll be enough to get her to understand the depths of what I feel for her, but I know there's no better way to tell her than through this.

"I want you to hear something," I say.

I navigate to my email and click on the most recent file that Blue sent me after our last session. I click on it and set my phone down on the music stand, the song starting to play.

This song took me months to write, longer than anything else because I couldn't find the right words. I couldn't capture the extraordinary emotions that were deep in my chest. Until it all just fell together. A song about love and hope and finding yourself while falling fast and hard for an incredible woman.

The last notes of the song fade out and the room is blanketed in silence again.

"This is the first love song I've ever written about someone in particular," I pause. "It's about you. I know I said that I would go at your pace, and I'm still committed to doing that, but I never want you to question how I feel about you Laila. I'm not asking you to be where I'm at, all I'm asking is for you to trust me."

She flicks her eyes up to meet mine and I see all of her, the depths of herself that she keeps locked away, laid bare for me to see.

Laila shifts subtly, a gentle rock forward of her hips, and I watch as the look in her eyes transforms to lust.

I lean forward and press my lips to hers, a gentle press that quickly turns frenzied. Our tongues duel as the intensity of our kiss continues to rise. Laila grinds into the growing swell of my dick and a deep low groan escapes my lips. M

y hands travel under the hem of the oversized shirt Laila had thrown on and cup both of her breasts, running my thumbs over her hardened nipples causing her to shudder. Laila pulls at the shirt, tugging it over her head and tossing it somewhere on the floor.

I take a moment to take her in, the swell of her breasts and the softness of her stomach, her beautiful body bare on top of me. The sun is just starting to rise and it covers her skin in a beautiful glow.

I dip my head and take one of Laila's nipples into my mouth. She places her hand on the back of my neck, holding me to her as I lick and suck and tug on her breast. I switch to the other breast giving it equal treatment drawing a pleasure filled whimper from Laila.

I release her nipple with a satisfying pop and kiss my way back up her body, easing my way up her shoulder and neck until I capture her lips again. She starts to writhe under me and I adjust her slightly so she's no longer sitting on both of my legs but now just one. I break our kiss and watch as Laila grinds her pussy on my thigh, her eyes closed, one arm braced on my shoulder, using me to get the friction she's seeking.

I hum. "There you go baby. Use me."

After a few more rotations of her hips, her movements slow and I grip her thighs, holding her as I stand and walk back to my bedroom. I place her down on the bed and spread open her legs, my thumb finding her clit and applying firm pressure. She squirms and tries to back away from me, but I place my other hand on her hip and hold her in place.

I press two fingers to her entrance and her wetness allows them to glide right in. I start moving them in and out of her slowly, pulling them nearly all the way out before sinking back in to my knuckles.

"More," Laila whines and I oblige, increasing my pace and causing her pussy to tighten.

I curl my fingers up, caressing the inside of her pussy and I feel as she reaches closer and closer to the edge.

"That's it, baby girl," I say. "Make a mess all over me."

Seconds later she erupts, her body jerking as her orgasm rips through her.

I ease my fingers out of her and pull my shorts and boxers down together in one swift motion. I place my hands under Laila's thighs and tug her to the edge of the bed.

I rub the head of my dick through her slick folds before I push into her, the blissful warmth and wetness of her pussy greeting me. I lean down to place a kiss on her lips. As we pull apart Laila whispers, "I do trust you."

25
Sonny

If you love something, set it free.

That proverb feels the most relevant on days like today. Days where I share a little piece of me with the world. Today it's this listening party followed by a midnight release of one song. A single, whose purpose is to build buzz and hype surrounding the upcoming album.

We've been teasing it for weeks, releasing snippets, sharing parts of my studio sessions, all of the things, and the reception has been generally good. That early positive reception doesn't dull the doubt that tries to sneak in and tell me that this release will be a failure, that I'm a failure.

The ability to release music that I actually enjoy creating and is a greater representation of who I am is an amazing privilege that I don't take for granted. I made these songs for me, more so than I have anything else that I have ever released. Yet I would be lying if I said that I didn't want others to enjoy it too, that I don't pray for success to drown out the noise that my brain tries to make me believe is fact. For that, only time will tell.

From the very beginning, the mood that I wanted this album to exude has been connection. Not only do I want my fans to feel more connected to me, the real me, but I also wanted to feel more connected to them. One of the best ways I could think of to attain the latter was through events with smaller crowds.

That desire spawned the idea of pop up listening parties. Spontaneous, low cost events across the country to share some of the songs from the album and some that didn't make the final cut.

"I thought I might find you out here."

I smile at the sound of her voice. I don't open my eyes until I hear her footsteps stop, coming to stand right beside me. Finally I open my eyes and look over at Laila. Amusement shines in her deep brown irises, a smirk on her lips.

"I'm that predictable huh?"

"Maybe just a little."

Laila pushes up on her toes to give me a kiss. She intends for it to be a peck, a soft press of her lips to mine, but when she pulls away I wrap my arm around her waist and pull her back to me. I place another kiss to her lips, and slide my hand down to squeeze her ass.

"Are you nervous?" Laila asks.

"A little bit," I reply honestly. "I'm not usually but this feels so-"

"Vulnerable?" Laila says, filling in the word for me.

I nod. "Yeah. It's a lot easier to not be worried when you're singing about shit that doesn't matter. If people didn't like it, it wasn't a big deal, but this is sharing a piece of me and I want it to be received well."

"It will."

She says it definitively, leaving no room for the doubt I've previously allowed to weasel its way in.

"Thank you."

"OH MY GOD, SONNY!"

A shrill woman's voice startles us both. I use my left arm to maneuver Laila behind me, putting her between me and the wall of the building and shielding her from the woman that's approaching us.

I look past her to see where she could have possibly come from when this area was supposed to be blocked off and secure. I don't see anything off putting and it seems like she's the only one who's found her way back here.

"I'm Carly and I absolutely *LOVE* you and your music. I can't believe I'm actually seeing you in person!"

"Are you here for the event?" I ask, still trying to figure out where she came from.

"I wish," the woman says, sticking her bottom lip out in a pout. "I tried to get a ticket but they sold out so fast."

"Yeah, it surprised us all. We'll be doing more events in the future though-, so maybe you'll be able to come to the next one."

"Yeah, but you probably have at least one extra ticket right?"

The woman tucks a piece of her light brown hair behind her ear and bats her blue eyes, probably thinking that will help her get what she's seeking.

I shake my head. "I'm not in charge of the tickets and unfortunately we're all sold out."

"Yes, but they work for you. I'm sure they could find one more ticket if you asked them to."

"It doesn't really work like that-, but if I could I would," I lie, hoping that she'll take no for an answer.

I don't want this situation to escalate, especially not with Laila here. I try to keep my voice light while I talk to her, hoping that if I stay cordial she'll leave quickly.

"Well, can I have a picture then at least?" the girl asks, preparing to raise her phone to take a selfie.

I clench my teeth. I was hoping that she wouldn't ask for that, knowing that my denial of her request could lead to this situation becoming unpleasant.

"I'm sorry," I say. "I'm not taking pictures right now."

The girl frowns. "It's just one quick picture and you won't even give me that."

Early on in my career I set the boundary that I wouldn't take pictures with people who saw me while I was just out and about in public. At an event or during a meet and greet, absolutely, but anything outside of that, no.

I wanted to establish some separation between me and my fans for both my safety and as a form of respect to me as a human and not just an entertainer. Since I set the precedent early, I rarely get approached for photos.

"I'm sorry," I repeat.

"Yo Sonny -"

Xavier steps out from the building, the rest of his sentence left unfinished. He takes a second to assess the scene between me and the woman before he steps in to put an end to it.

"You aren't supposed to be here ma'am," Xavier says, stepping towards the woman. "I'm going to have to ask you to leave."

"What? No!" the woman shouts. "Sonny was going to get me a ticket to the show tonight. I'm his biggest fan!"

"No he's not," Xavier says.

"This is how you treat your supporters?" the woman yells as Xavier takes her arm and starts leading her away. Once they're no longer close I turn to Laila.

"Hey, are you okay?"

She nods, but I can tell that interaction made her uncomfortable, her body tense and eyes focused on the direction that Xavier and the woman went.

"Let's go back inside," I say.

I take her hand in mine, walking to the door and pulling it open for her to enter first. We make our way to the dressing room and

Xavier is already standing there. Laila goes in and I stop in the doorway.

"Everything handled?" I ask.

"I handed her off to one of the other guys. She's off the premises and they're doing another walk around to make sure no one else can get through."

"Thank you," I say and start to walk into the room when Xavier puts a hand out to stop me.

"You want to tell me why you were out there without eyes?" Xavier asks.

"I just needed a minute."

Xavier shakes his head. "Doesn't work that way, boss."

"I know, my fault."

More security was hired for this event, new guys who I hadn't worked with before. Xavier had been talking to some of the other security guards when I slipped away. One of the guys had started to follow me outside but I waved him off, just wanting a minute alone. Xavier would've never listened to that command-, but this guy obeyed my request without any protest.

"It won't happen again. You need security with you whether you want it or not," Xavier says, his voice stern. "Your safety isn't something we can play with. I'm not gonna be the one that has to tell your OG that something happened to her son on my watch."

***

There's an excited, anticipatory energy in the room, even with only a little over a hundred people in attendance. The lights are turned down low to create a calm, comfortable environment. The first thing that I notice is that I can see the crowd, like really see them and their details. They aren't just blobs of light that all mesh together like how it is when you perform on a larger scale.

Rows of chairs are lined up in a half circle around where I'm standing. Every seat filled and all eyes on me as I bring the mic in my hand to my mouth and begin to speak.

"I just want to start out by saying thank you to all of you for coming out tonight."

The room erupts into cheers and claps and I pause, smiling, taking it all in.

When the room quiets, I continue. "I feel so very blessed to be able to have this experience with y'all. Without you I wouldn't be able to do what I love. I'm eternally grateful for all the support I've been shown over the years and that you took time out of your day to be here tonight."

"Almost four years ago, I met someone and one of the first things they said to me was that I was an asshole."

Snickers erupt through the room.

"Y'all think it's funny but I'm being for real," I say, chuckling myself. "But she was right, I was an asshole. I had strayed so far from the man I wanted to be, too caught up in trying to reach the highest highs that I lost myself in the process."

The crowd hums, nods and murmurs of understanding flow through the space. I look around, taking everyone in but also scanning, searching for a set of deep brown eyes that I have become intimately familiar with. The beautiful woman that turned my world upside down in the best way possible.

She's in the very back of the room standing near the mixing booth with Morgan. I'm sure the choice is meant to make her inconspicuous and for the other people in the room, it probably is. For me, Laila is a light that can never be dimmed or hidden. She may not want the attention of everyone else in the room, but she'll always have mine.

I tear my gaze away from her and engage back with the crowd as I walk back and forth in the small space, continuing to talk.

"That conversation was the wake up call that I needed.. These songs are heartfelt and real and -" I pause, glancing around the room. "Vulnerable. I hope you enjoy. Thank you."

***

My phone is flooded with notifications. An overwhelming amount of missed calls and texts from friends and family. Two notifications catch my attention immediately, three back to back calls from Morgan followed by a text message.

Morgan

Call me back asap.

I ignore the rest of the notifications, tapping on the missed call from Morgan to call her back.

"Have you been on social media yet?" Morgan asks when the call connects.

I furrow my brows in confusion. "Nah, not yet I just woke up. I saw your message and called you. Why? Is the song performing badly?"

"No, it's not that."

I can tell simply from the tone of Morgan's voice that something is wrong.

"Then what is it?"

"Someone posted photos of you and Laila together from last night along with a bunch of unkind things to say about the both of you."

My stomach drops at her words. "Fuck."

"I need you to stay off social media for right now. I've already scheduled a meeting with the rest of the team to figure out the best way to address this."

"I need to see the photo."

"Sonny, I don't think that's a good idea. Seeing the photos won't change anything and we need to focus on establishing a game plan right now."

I can count on one hand the number of times I've gone against Morgan's advice during the time that we've worked together. It's her job to manage me and she does it well. But this, this I can't agree to.

"I respect your opinion a lot, you know that, but this is about Laila. I can't be in the dark on this."

Morgan lets out a deep sigh. "You really aren't going to let this go are you?"

"No. I'm not."

There's a long pause of silence before she speaks again. "Fine. I just sent it to you."

I pull the phone away from my ear and open the message Morgan just sent me.

The photos are grainy, clearly taken from a good distance away but zoomed in. The first is just me standing outside with my eyes closed and the rest are from after Laila came outside with me.

For the most part, in the photos Laila is covered. My body shields hers from the camera so only a small fraction of her side profile is visible. Until the last one.

It was taken right after we broke apart from our kiss, my hand still on her ass. Even through the pixelation, Laila's entire face is on display.

"I gotta go."

"Sonny I know this isn't what either of you wanted-, but we need to talk with the rest of the team and-"

"And I will, but I need to talk to Laila first. I told her this wouldn't happen and here it is. I have to talk to her."

Before Morgan can even respond I end the call, navigating to Laila's contact and pressing the button to initiate a FaceTime. The call rings and rings but she never answers.

26
Sonny

me

Laila please answer the phone

me

I didn't know she took those pictures. Morgan is working now to get them taken down

me

Please talk to me. I'm so sorry this happened

me

I have the event in Detroit tonight but I'll be back tomorrow. I'll have my phone so if you want to talk I'm here.

27
Laila

ZARA AND I CLINK our glasses together before we tap them on the bar and then down our shots. I grimace at the burn of the liquor and then take a sip of my mixed drink to chase it.

"Another round?" I ask.

"Listen, I'm all for you having a good time," Zara says. "But drowning yourself in liquor isn't going to make you feel better about Sonny, babe."

I frown. "It's not about him."

Zara rolls her eyes at me and in a joking voice says, "Lie detector has determined that's a lie. Try again."

"It's not," I argue. "You're the one who always wants me to come out and have fun, and here I am."

"I do, but I also want you to be happy and not just here because you're trying to avoid thinking about that man that you're mad at."

"I'm not mad at him," I say, sighing. "I'm just... sad. I feel like we were in this little bubble and then someone came and popped it, and now we're out in the open for all to see."

"It doesn't have to be that way. There are plenty of celebrities who don't share all their business and Sonny wasn't one of them to begin with."

"Maybe," I reply, noncommittally.

Zara wants to argue more with me but she doesn't. Instead she turns and flags the bartender down and orders us more shots of vodka.

Deep down, I know she's right because truthfully I don't want to be here. I want to be able to go back to two weeks ago before everything changed. But I can't and I couldn't stand one more second of wallowing in my apartment so a night out at Oasis with vodka shots and Moscow Mules was the next logical option in my eyes. It's been almost two weeks since those pictures and articles came out and I feel like I've only just now been able to come up for air after being blindsided seeing my face all over the media.

I deleted all social media off my phone after one late night of reading mean comments about myself and besides work, I haven't left my apartment until now. Tonight I'm determined not to think about any of it. I just want to have some fun.

We stay by the bar instead of finding seating somewhere else tonight. It's not very busy and the vibes are good. We talk and drink and I finally start to feel myself relax and enjoy the night. Zara and I decide to take another round of shots, the last ones before we plan to call it a night.

"Next round is on me," a voice says from my left.

I turn to see who is speaking to us and annoyance immediately sparks when I see who it is.

Devin is sitting on the stool next to me with a smirk on his face, a glass of Jack and Coke most likely, in his hand.

"I'm actually done for the night, so no thanks," I say.

"Let me pick up your tab then."

"No."

I flick my hair over my shoulder and turn back to Zara prepared to tell her that I'm ready to leave when Devin interjects again, his tone filled with condescension.

"It's just a drink Laila. No big deal."

"I'm not interested," I say.

"Why are you even here?" Zara cuts in. "Don't you have a baby you need to be tending to."

"I'm here talking to Laila," he says.

"We don't have shit to talk about," I reply.

Devin takes a sip of his drink. "You're fucking a new nigga and think you're all that now huh? Only washed up singers do it for you now."

"Get the fuck out my face Devin."

Devin holds up his hands in mock surrender. "I was just trying to be nice, no need to be so hostile."

"If you think that's hostile you haven't seen anything yet. Why don't you go on and bother someone else."

"I was just being nice and offering to get you a drink. Didn't realize that was such a problem."

I feel Bryce's presence before he even speaks. The warmth of his body near mine brings goosebumps to my arms, his cologne in my nostrils so familiar.

"Your ears must need to be checked because you clearly can't take a hint," Bryce says to Devin. "I think it's time for you to get up outta here."

Devin chuckles and takes a sip from his drink. "Good thing I didn't ask what you thought."

"You've clearly misunderstood. It wasn't a suggestion," Bryce says.

Xavier comes up behind Devin with another man who must be security. The security guard taps him on the shoulder and says something low in his ear.

"What I'm getting asked to leave over a bitch I was trying to be nice to?" Devin says, his voice exasperated as if I was the one who did something to him.

Before the words have even fully left his mouth, I toss the contents of my glass in Devin's direction. Most of the liquid hits him square in the chest, soaking his shirt. He jumps up and starts yelling, cursing at me but I'm already walking away, moving as fast as my legs will take me because all of this is just too much.

Instead of heading towards the exit, I find myself down one of the service hallways, the lights dim and the walls black, an area clearly not meant for patrons to be in. I turn on my heel and face Bryce who's been only a few paces behind me this whole time.

"Are you following me now?"

"You're in my lounge, but you think I'm the one following you?"

I let out an exasperated sigh, ready to turn around and get out of here when Bryce stops me, grabbing my arm. "To answer your question, no. Tristan had some things that he wanted me to look over tonight. He had some opportunities that he thought I might be interested in investing in. I was headed out when I saw that nigga all in your face. I went over to make sure you were good."

"You didn't need to do that."

"If you think that when I see another nigga, talking crazy in my girl's face and I'm not gonna step in then you've got it all wrong," Bryce says shaking his head.

"Well I'm sure it gave all the blogs and news outlets even more to talk about."

"Fuck them and what they have to say," he says. "It doesn't matter."

"That's so easy for you to say," I reply. "You're not the one getting vile shit said about them, getting called a whore and a gold digger for even being associated with you."

Bryce closes the small distance between us and brings his hands up to hold the sides of my face.

"I'm sorry," he says, holding the sides of my face. "You don't deserve to have your privacy violated like that-, or for people to think it's okay to say horrible things about you. You told me your boundaries and I didn't do enough to protect them. I won't make that same mistake again."

I force myself to take a step back, my mind filled with conflicting emotions because as much as I want to let Bryce in, it all feels like too much, too vulnerable. Bryce's hands fall from my face and he shoves his hands in his pockets.

"I think we both need to take some time to figure this all out," I say, looking down at my feet.

"I think that you're using that as an excuse to push me away."

I don't have a response for that, not a good one, anyway. I *am* pushing him away. It's easier than facing all the emotions that have been welling up inside of me, the hard parts that are uncomfortable to tackle. It's easier to simply walk away.

I push past Bryce to walk back the way I came. "I gotta go find Zara."

I'm almost at the end of the hallway when I hear Bryce's voice behind me. "I don't need time to figure anything out. I want you and I'm not going to let anything get in the way of that, even your doubts."

28
Laila

CASS CONNECTS HER PHONE to the speaker in *Lovely Day's* shipping room. She turns the volume down to background noise level before she joins me at the long table that we use to pack orders.

Packing and managing orders, making sure they go out when they are supposed to is usually handled by Reagan and Stella. Both of them are out on vacation this week, Stella for a bachelorette trip and Reagan for her birthday. Cass and I decided to do some of the packing while they're gone so the orders don't pile up.

When I first started working at *Lovely Day* my senior year of college, it was only me and Cass. At that time I was more of an assistant than anything else and did anything that needed to be done for the business-, and usually one of those things was packing orders. It feels very full circle to be packing orders with her again. I'm even recording some behind the scenes footage to be able to post on our socials, just like I would do back then.

We pack orders, working in tandem with each other, finding a rhythm that works efficiently. She picks the items from the shelves of inventory and places them into a bin with the packing slip and hands them off to me. From there, I pack the boxes, adding tissue paper and the thank you note before taping the box closed.

I reach for the next order bin but immediately stop when a sharp pain occurs in my lower abdomen. I groan and place my hand where the pain is coming from, applying pressure to try to alleviate the pain.

"Are you okay?" Cass asks, a concerned look on her face.

I close my eyes and focus on breathing through the pain until it subsides, turning into a dull ache.

"Yeah it's just cramps," I reply. "My period was supposed to start two days ago, but my body is drawing out the suffering this month."

"Oh the joys of being a woman," Cass says.

She places a shipping label on the box that she just finished packing, closing it up with tape. "You don't have to stay if you aren't feeling well, you know that."

"I know, but I want to help get these orders out before the weekend. I'll be cuddled up with my heating pad all day tomorrow while I work from home."

"You know what always gets my period to start?" Cass asks.

"What?"

"Taking a pregnancy test."

"You can't be for real." I say.

"I'm so serious," she says. "Anytime my period is later than I expect it to be, I take a test and boom within a few hours, maybe a day max, my period starts."

I look at her skeptically. "I don't know. I have all the symptoms I usually have before my period starts so I know it's on its way."

"Of course, but just know if you want to speed up the arrival, my trick does it every time."

We continue packing orders, doing a mixture of singing along to the songs playing through the speaker and catching up. We have made it a little over three quarters of the way through the orders we wanted to fulfill today when Cass's phone starts to ring. She sets down the order that she was working on and picks up her phone, smiling at the name of the caller. From the way she answers the phone I know it's Cyrus. She walks out of the room, talking to him, a joyfulness in her tone that only he brings out of her that I'm so happy she gets to experience.

While she's gone my cramps intensify causing more discomfort, so much so that I can't just ignore them like I've been trying to do. I finish packing the body butters for the last order that I have and then I take a break, sitting down in one of the nearby chairs.

My eyes are squeezed shut and I'm breathing through another intense cramp when Cass comes back.

"Girl, go home," she says when she sees me.

This time I don't even bother arguing with her, both because it would be futile and also because I don't actually feel good. We made a decent sized dent in our orders and that's good enough for me today.

I pick up my things from my desk, my purse and the fresh bouquet of flowers that was delivered this morning. Bryce has continued to send me flowers frequently. Roses, peonies, hydrangeas, always something different. Today its white roses.

I usually leave them on my desk to enjoy while at work but I won't be working in the office for a few days, so I opt to take them home with me. I call a rideshare to go home because at this moment I don't have the energy for walking or taking public transportation and just want to get to my bed and heating pad as quickly as possible. The driver comes after a few minutes and the ride is quick and uneventful, just what I needed.

When I get out of the car, thanking the driver as I close the door, I see the pharmacy that's across the street from my building. I take a second to debate whether or not I should take Cass's advice.

Another twinge of pain hits my lower abdomen causing me to wince.

Fuck it why not.

I leave the vase of flowers in the lobby of my building while I go to the pharmacy, freeing my arms from carrying them to the store with me

As I enter the store, I grab a handbasket and walk first to the snack aisle. I let my stomach guide me as I grab things. Chocolate and sour gummy worms and salt and vinegar chips all find their way into my basket before I move on. A couple aisles over, next to the tampons and the condoms are the pregnancy tests.

I've never paid much attention to pregnancy tests before. The two very full shelves with so many different options immediately overwhelms me.

Digital. Not digital. Early detection. Advanced early result. The blue brand. The pink brand. Pluses and minuses and lines and smiley faces. So many different choices for one product.

I grab one at random, hoping that Cass's trick isn't brand specific. I take my items to self checkout, setting the basket on the designated space next to the register. I do a double take when I scan the pregnancy test box, startled at the price of something that I only intend to pee on. I toss it into the bag with the rest of my things and then take out my card to pay. I grab the mile long receipt after it prints out and leave the store, stuffing it into the bag with my items.

In my apartment, I hang my purse on the hook by the door and drop the bag of things I bought from the pharmacy on the kitchen counter along with the flowers. I

go to my bathroom and turn on my shower to warm it up while I strip out of my clothes. TI don't bother reading the instructions. It should be as simple as peeing on the stick right? I rip the box open and pull out one of the tests, taking the top off before sitting down to take the test. I place the test on the counter next to the sink, wash my hands and then turn on the shower water to warm it up.

The warmth of the shower water hitting my skin feels amazing and helps soothe the discomfort that I've been feeling through the day. I stand under the water for much longer than necessary before I actually start the process of cleaning my body.

Eventually I turn off the water and dry off, moisturizing and then putting on the robe hanging from my bathroom door. As I slip my arms into the second sleeve, my eye catches the pregnancy test on the counter. I left it face up and on the test is something I never expected.

Two pink lines.

One much fainter than the other but still visibly there.

No.

I go to my kitchen, grabbing a glass from the cabinet and filling it with water. I chug the whole glass, hoping it will fill my bladder quickly so that I can take the other test because the first one was clearly wrong.

I pace back and forth in my bathroom until I have the smallest inkling that I have something to use for the test. I set the test down on the counter and wash my hands. A little clock appears on the test.. I brace myself on the counter, my eyes fixated on the little window on the test as I anxiously wait for it to tell me that the first one was just faulty. My eyes burn as I watch the test until the little clock disappears and something else takes its place.

yes +

29
Sonny

For my first interview in half a decade, Morgan wanted to come back with a bang which meant starting with the best. In this instance, the best is Danika Riley. Danika is one of the most popular interviewers in the game. Her backlog of guests on her show, *Let's Catch Up,* is not only extensive but also diverse. She sits down with everyone from professional athletes to actors to entertainers.

The stage is set up to feel cozy. Two large armchairs facing each other with a side table in between us with branded mugs filled with water. A plush rug under our feet and plants in the background. Everything in a color scheme of creams and browns and olive greens to help with the impression that Danika and her guest are old friends catching up with each other and not on a set with cameras and crew all around.

"Are you ready?" Danika asks when her hair and makeup team is done with their final touch ups.

I'm not. I don't want to be here today. I even told Morgan to cancel my appearance but she flat out refused. She told me that I owed it to myself and to the album to give it everything that I had to make it successful. I could spend the rest of the day holed up in my place, sad, but first I had to do the work. She was right and so here I am on set, poised with a microphone in front of me.

I nod and smile. "Yeah, let's do it."

A moment later the cameras start rolling.

"Sonny, it's so good to see you. How are you doing?" Danika asks, her voice chipper.

"I'm doing really well. Thank you for having me."

"You've been out of the spotlight for some time now, some even thought that your career was done. How does it feel to be back?"

"It doesn't feel like I'm 'back' because I don't feel like I left," I say. "Even though I wasn't sharing it or performing, I never stopped creating, making music never stopped being a part of me. Now it just feels like I can share it with the world again and I'm forever grateful for that opportunity."

"So all this time you've been writing songs still?"

I chuckle. "Yeah, as crazy as it may sound, I've been writing songs since I was a teenager. I don't really remember what it's like to not have lyrics floating around in my head most days."

"And one of those songs turned into your latest release, *Love Notes*. It's been rapidly climbing the charts since your surprise release and is now in competition with some of your previous songs in initial popularity. Can you tell us a little about your inspiration for *Love Notes*.

"*Love Notes* is all about self love, doing what's best for you even if others think you shouldn't. It's about putting yourself first. While working with my team to figure out what song I wanted to release first, this one always stuck out to me because I feel like it embodies the vibe and the message that I want to portray for the entire album."

"That's amazing," Danika says. "Long time fans of yours know that you were previously signed to a label and now you've chosen to be independent. Can you tell us more about how you came to that decision?"

"I was young when I signed my deal and over the course of it, I grew not only as an artist but also as a man. I lost myself a little bit and I needed time to figure out what the journey forward looked like for me. I try my hardest not to live life with regrets because I wouldn't be where I am now without the things I've been through, the good and the bad. I couldn't find anywhere that felt like a good fit for me so I decided to take the chance on myself and release on my own."

"Speaking of your new release, what does it feel like after nearly half a decade away?"

"Exhilarating," I reply easily. "But also terrifying and emotional."

"So it's safe to say you're bringing a new energy with this album," Danika says with a chuckle.

"Absolutely. I want this next chapter of my life to feel more authentic to who I am as a person and I hope that's reflected in not only this next album but all my future work."

"So I was doing my research," Danika says. "And in all the things I could find about you, you've never told the story of your name. How did you decide on Sonny?"

I pick up the mug and take a sip of water.

"My father coached football for years and when I was little I was always out on the field with him. I was like his shadow and all the guys embraced me as a part of the team but no one ever called me Bryce, my real name. They always said 'Coach's son' and then that got shortened to 'son' and then just 'Sonny' and 'Sonny' stuck as a nickname for me ever since."

"Thank you for sharing that with us," Danika says with a soft smile.

The interview continues on with Danika asking other personal and professional questions, most of them being things that Morgan and I prepped for. Until the one topic that I hoped she wouldn't ask me about.

"Notably, you are rarely seen publicly linked to a woman. Until recently, the closest had been your rumored relationship with artist, Essence. What can you tell us about your new boo?"

I look over at Morgan who's standing on the sidelines of the set, questioning with my eyes whether she knew this topic would be discussed or not. She shakes her head, fury in her eyes on my behalf.

Morgan and I had extensive conversations about how I didn't want to use my relationship with Laila as a marketing tactic.

The show isn't live so I know this part will be edited out post production.

"Essence is a great person to work with but it has only ever been that, nothing more. As for my current relationship, that isn't something that I really want to speak on."

"Hmmm, so this is just going to stay your little secret."

"No, not at all," I say. "A secret implies something to hide and nothing about my relationship is a secret but we do want to be private. She didn't ask to be thrust into the spotlight, she isn't seeking fame, and that shouldn't have to change simply because she chooses to be with me. Everyone deserves their privacy."

Danika turns to the camera for a dramatic effect. "Oh he's serious serious y'all"

With that, Danika takes the hint and moves on to another topic.

30
Sonny

I FAKE LEFT ON my defender and then step back, bring the ball up and take my shot. The ball bounces off the rim and Malik rebounds it, passing it to one of his teammates before it gets passed back to him for an easy layup.

Game point.

I make my way over to the sideline, grabbing my towel and wiping the sweat off my face.

"You aight, man? I don't think I've seen you play that bad since the fifth grade," Chris says chuckling, his tone light.

I send a glare in his direction as I grab my duffel bag and start packing my things up to leave.

He raises his hands in mock surrender. "I'm just telling it how I see it."

He wasn't wrong, I *had* played like shit today, missing nearly all my shots and slow on getting rebounds.

"I'm good," I say, ignoring his comment.

Chris reached out the day the pictures surfaced of me and Laila. He congratulated me on the release of my single and also told me that he was always available if I needed to talk.

"I meant what I said before," he says, the humor gone from his voice. "I'm here if you need me."

"Appreciate it," I say, dapping him up.

I toss a hand in goodbye to the rest of the group before I leave the gym.

Xavier has already brought the car up to the door of the building so I easily slide into the passenger seat and he drives me back to my place. After the photo leak, I've been keeping security around me more than I used to.

I drop my duffel bag by the door, and toe out of my shoes. I make it a few steps into the living room before I stop mid step.

Laila is curled up on my couch, a blanket wrapped tightly around her as she sleeps. I'm shocked at her presence, especially since our communication has been nonexistent except one text telling me that she needed space.

I walk over to the couch and smile when I hear her soft snores. I gently run a finger down her cheek and she doesn't stir.

Seeing her again in my space reminds me just how much I've missed her. I respected that she needed space but I would be lying if I said that it was easy to keep my distance from her. No good would have come from me putting my own feelings over hers, so like I told her I would before, I followed her lead.

I decide to let her sleep, not wanting to wake her up from a nap that is clearly much needed. I leave the living room and go to my bathroom, turning on the hot water in the shower to wash off all the sweat and stink from playing ball this morning.

After I've showered and moisturized, I go back out to the living room and find Laila in the same position as I left her. I sit down in the spot next to her head and I'm struck by how damn gorgeous she is. I catch myself watching her sleep for way too long again before I take out my phone to scroll until she wakes up.

Laila opens her eyes and sits up, disoriented for a moment before her gaze lands on me.

"Hey," I say softly.

"Hey."

Quiet falls over the room as we both take each other in.

Laila sinks her teeth into her bottom lip and it takes everything in me to keep my hands to myself, to not try to swoop in and erase all the hurt and uncertainty in her eyes.

"I'm sorry that I'm here unannounced. I thought you would be home but then you weren't and I didn't want to leave without talking to you. So I decided to wait for you but I was so tired that I guess I fell asleep."

Laila rambles a clear sign of her nerves and I hate that she even feels the need to explain herself to me.

I shake my head. "You have that key for a reason. It has always been yours to freely use."

"I know but I just -"

I don't let her finish that sentence, wrapping my arms around her and pulling her into me, unable to fight the urge to have her in my arms any longer.

She lays her head on my chest, the sweet scent of her shampoo flooding my nostrils. I feel her relax into me, the rhythm of her breaths slowing as her nerves ease.

"The pictures have been taken down," I say, quietly. "And Morgan and my team are putting more things in place to make sure that your privacy is respected in all aspects when it comes to being around me. I'm sorry that this happened and I promise to do everything in my power to make sure that it doesn't happen again."

"Thank you," Laila murmurs, her voice small. "I just needed some time to process everything."

"I want you to feel comfortable talking to me. I don't want you to feel like you need to retreat into yourself when things get hard."

"It's been just me for so long. Yes I have Zara and my other friends but I never wanted to put the weight of what I'm dealing with on them, so I have always just figured it out on my own."

"Lean on me," I say. "Let me hold some of the weight you've been carrying for so long. You don't have to do it all by yourself."

"It felt like a cruel joke," Laila says. "I had finally let myself fall for you and then my worst fear came to pass. It felt like some sort of punishment."

"Is that how you still feel?"

Laila sits up and tugs the abandoned blanket back around her body.

"No, but then I started reading the comments and I know I shouldn't have but everyone had such nasty things to say and it started to make me second guess myself. They made me second guess if I had just made it all up in my head."

I cup Laila's chin, forcing her to look at me as I speak my next words. "Nothing anyone else can say will ever come between you and me unless we let it. I've been going crazy without you around and unless *you* tell me otherwise, I'm not going anywhere."

Laila sniffles and tears well up in her eyes. I pull her back to me and she sobs into my chest. Eventually her cries slow to sniffles and I continue to hold her, rubbing her back in circles to try to bring her some comfort.

"Baby, tell me what's wrong," I say.

"I -," she starts, her voice shaky. "I'm pregnant."

My hand stills on her back, stunned by her words.

Pregnant.

Of all of the things I thought she might say, this wasn't even on the list. We hadn't been as careful as we could have been but we hadn't been totally reckless either.

"I thought-"

"I am," Laila says, answering the thought that I wasn't able to fully get out. "I have an IUD but for whatever reason it didn't work."

"Don't cry, baby," I say, wiping away the tears that have streaked down her face. "How long have you known?"

"Like a week and a half," Laila sniffles. "I went to the doctor a few days ago and did a blood test and it confirmed it."

"Are you okay?"

Laila shrugs. "My next appointment is in a couple of weeks."

"But how do *you* feel?" I ask, being more specific with my question.

Her shoulders sag. "Not good. I'm so tired all the time no matter how much sleep I've gotten. I also have had a lot of cramping, my doctor said that that is a common symptom that women have but it's so uncomfortable."

I kiss the top of her head. "I'm sorry that you've been dealing with this alone. We'll figure it out together, okay?"

"Okay."

Laila spends the rest of the day with me. We spend most of it on the couch together watching the last season of her show. It's mostly me watching because Laila's fatigue causes her to go in and out of sleep.

31
Laila

Something is wrong.

A sharp pain wakes me from my sleep. Another piercing jab hits the same spot and I sit up, clutching my right side.

I make my way to the en suite to relieve my bladder and when I sit down, blood in my panties stares back at me. It is bright red in color and my stomach drops immediately when I notice its presence.

After I finish cleaning myself up, I slide down onto the floor, the cool tiles on the back of my thighs. Blood rushes in my ears and I feel nothing but numbness.

I'm not sure how long I've been sitting on the floor when Bryce finds me. He sits down in front of me, taking my hands in his.

He doesn't ask me to talk or to tell him what's wrong, he just sits there with me, rubbing his thumbs over the backs of my hands while I focus on the newly difficult task of bringing air into my lungs.

"I'm bleeding," I whisper, barely able to get the words out.

He pulls me into him, and holds me. My head rests on his chest and I can hear the rhythmic thumping of his heartbeat.

Bryce places a kiss on my forehead. "Let me make some quick calls and then we'll go get you checked out."

He helps me to my feet and walks me back into the bedroom before he grabs his phone and leaves the room. I go to the closet to find a change of clothes and grab one of the first things I see, a cozy matching sweat set. When I am done changing, I see Bryce waiting for me at the doorway to the bedroom. He takes my hand and we head to the car together.

We enter the emergency room through a back entrance and we're led straight to a private room. A nurse hands me a gown to change into and then comes back a few minutes later to take my vitals.

"The doctor will be in with you shortly," the nurse says as she finishes jotting down my blood pressure.

The overhead lighting of the hospital is so bright, deeply contrasting with the fact that it's the middle of the night. My hands twist restlessly in my lap as I sit in the bed and I stare directly at my sock clad feet, zoning out.

It isn't a long wait before there are two taps on the door signifying someone entering. A Black doctor with honey colored skin wearing navy blue scrubs walks in.

"Hi sweetheart," she says with a thick southern accent. "I'm Doctor Carter and I'm going to be taking care of you. Can you tell me a little bit more about what brought you in tonight?"

She listens intently, nodding her head as I tell her everything that I've been experiencing.

"The doctor's office told me that my symptoms weren't abnormal and I shouldn't worry, but it just doesn't feel right."

My voice cracks as I finish talking. I close my eyes and take a deep breath to try to steady myself.

Dr. Carter rests her hand on mine. "You did the right thing. We're going to get this figured out, okay?"

"Based on the date of your last menstrual cycle that's in your chart, you're about six and a half weeks along. I would like to do an ultrasound to see what's going on," Dr. Carter says, her voice gentle. "Do you want us to clear the room?"

I look over at Bryce. He's sitting in a chair behind the doctor, his elbows propped on his knees and his hands clasped together. He's been quiet since the doctor walked in but I see that he's worried, concern etched all over his face. The mere thought of Bryce leaving the room causes my heart rate to uncomfortably quicken so I swiftly shake my head.

"No, I would like him to stay."

A nurse comes in with the ultrasound machine. She places a blanket over my lower half and instructs me to lay back and on how to place my legs.

Dr. Carter warns me that I may experience some discomfort before she applies lubricant to the wand and then begins the ultrasound.

Bryce stands next to me, on the opposite side of the bed from Dr. Carter. One of his hands holds mine and the other gently brushes the hair at my temple.

The air in the room is thick. It feels like all of us wait on bated breath as Dr. Carter moves the probe around and hits buttons on the machine. I try to gauge the severity of whatever is happening to me by her face but her expression is unreadable, a skill that has probably been purposely honed for years during her career but leaves me anxiously awaiting her findings.

Finally Dr. Carter turns to me and starts to explain. She points out different parts on the screen, pointing out how things should look versus how they actually look for me but my brain can't really make sense of anything on the grainy black and gray screen.

"Based on what I'm seeing, your pregnancy is ectopic. The baby is attached to your right fallopian tube. With your symptoms and the pain you've been experiencing, I'm worried about a possible rupture and I don't want to risk that. I think it's best for you to have surgery."

Dr. Carter explains the procedure and I try my best to listen and take in all the information that she's giving to me but I feel like my head's underwater and all the words are rushing past me without ever sinking in.

"Laila."

It's Bryce's voice that snaps me out of the mental fog that surrounds me. I look up at him

"Baby, the doctor wants to know if you have any questions."

I feel like I have whiplash. I had only just begun to wrap my mind around this pregnancy. The reality of it all just barely sinking in before this sudden hospital trip in the early hours of the morning on a random Tuesday.

My heart feels like it's been ripped out of my body but no, I don't have any questions.

32
Laila

THE HEAVENLY AROMA COMING from the kitchen causes my stomach to grumble. I haven't had much of an appetite, the concept of food wholly unappealing. When my stomach grumbles a second time, I toss the covers off and get out of bed to walk to the kitchen.

My steps still when I reach the end of the hallway and don't find Bryce in the kitchen but instead his mother stands at the stove, her back turned to me. I am about to turn and walk back to the bedroom but her voice stops me.

"He had a call he needed to take," she says, nodding her head toward the balcony.

I look over and I see Bryce with his headphones in, walking back and forth as he talks animatedly with someone on the other end of the call.

She hasn't turned around so I'm not sure how she knows I'm standing there but her words answer the question I hadn't said aloud.

"Come sit."

Her words are an invitation in the form of a command but the soft loving tone she uses has my feet moving before my mind has a moment to catch up. I close the distance to the bar stools and pull one out and sit down.

A host of ingredients are laid out on the counter. Fresh vegetables and herbs and potatoes amongst other things.

"What are you making?" I ask. "It smells amazing."

She turns and gives me a small smile. "This is what my children call "sick soup". It's a pot full of deliciousness that I always made when they weren't feeling well, physically or otherwise. A lot of bumps and bruises and broken hearts have been soothed by it."

I wrap my arms around my middle, hugging myself as I watch her make the soup. She adds ingredient after ingredient to her pot, not a measuring utensil in sight. She moves around the kitchen with the ease of someone who has no doubt in their skills, someone who knows that whatever they've tasked themselves with making will turn out exactly as they intended.

"I assume Bryce told you," I say, realizing that that's probably why she's here.

"He tells me a lot of things," she says. "But no, he didn't tell me anything. He just asked me if I would make him some soup because he wanted some comfort food for the both of you. So here I am."

"That's really sweet," I whisper.

"Oh it's nothing, darling. He's my son so I'll always do what I can."

Those words are what break me.

The ones that cause the tears that I haven't been able to shed, for myself, for my loss, for the part of me that I've had to harden to survive, to finally fall. First in slow streaks down my face and then a body wracking sob into my hands pressed to my face.

It only takes a moment for me to feel Bryce's mom's arms wrap around me. Her presence is comforting, while I cry so hard snot bubbles form and I'm hyperventilating.

She stands next to me and holds me, one hand rubbing my back in rhythmic circles. She doesn't try to ask me what's wrong or placate my feelings with empty positive words. She just lets me cry and cry until all the tears have left my body, leaving the beginnings of a headache in their wake.

"Do you want to talk about it?"

My gut reaction is to tell her 'no', to tell her that I'm fine, to ball up all my emotions and stuff them down inside of me like I have for my entire life. But something about this moment won't allow me to do that. Words spill out of me as I tell her everything, all the feelings that I've been holding in since I saw those two pink lines and everything else that's happened since.

"I didn't mean to get pregnant," I say, wiping my eyes with the cuffs of my sleeves. "I hadn't even made up my mind on what I wanted to do but I still feel so -"

I shake my head, unable to produce a word that could accurately describe all the emotions running through me right now.

"My husband and I lost two babies between Lauryn and Bryce," she says. "The first pregnancy was a surprise. We thought we were done having children after the girls. The second was planned. The circumstances didn't matter, they both hurt."

"Don't force your recovery. And I'm not just talking about the physical. Let yourself feel all that you need to and give yourself grace. It's okay to feel your pain. Sometimes we put all this pressure on ourselves to be okay and to snap back to normal but we shouldn't because pretending to be okay doesn't make actually being okay happen any faster than it was already going to."

The pot of soup starts to bubble higher, threatening to boil over and Bryce's mom swiftly goes over to tend to it. She adds the last few ingredients out on the counter and is slowly stirring the pot when Bryce comes back in.

He walks over to me and places a hand on the back of my stool. He looks between me and his mother, a question poised on his tongue when his mom speaks first.

"Your soup is just about done," Bryce's mom says, putting the last seasoning jar back into the cabinet. "I have to go pickup RJ from daycare."

She stirs the pot before placing a lid on it and adjusting the temperature. "Just let it simmer for a while longer and then it'll be all done." I'm unsure of the definition of 'a while' in this instance but I hope that Bryce knows so that we don't ruin her hard work.

She places a hand on my shoulder and gives it a squeeze. "Remember what I said and if you want to talk some more, I'm available any time."

I nod and give her a tight smile. Bryce walks her to the door, giving her a hug and a kiss on the cheek before she leaves and he closes the door behind her.

Bryce walks back to the kitchen and stands on the other side of the island. "Can I run you a bath?"

"Yes, I'd like that," I say, happy that I'm finally cleared to take them again after the surgery.

He holds out his hand to me and I take it as we walk to the bathroom together.

I lean against the vanity as I watch him begin to start the bath. He plugs the bottom and turns on the faucet to the massive freestanding tub in the center of the bathroom and then walks to the linen closet, opening the door.

A small smile comes to my face when I see him pull out a bag with *Lovely Day* packaging. It's one of our bath salt soaks, a newer item to our product line that was a part of our summer restock. I hadn't even known that he had bought it before seeing it right now. He sprinkles some of it into the water before returning the rest of the bag to where he retrieved it from.

As the water rises, he tests the temperature, running his fingers through the water and then adjusting the handles accordingly.

"Ready?" he asks, when he's satisfied with the water.

"Yes."

I allow him to help me undress, raising my arms and lifting my legs to shed my clothing. I take the few steps to the tub and stick one leg in and then the other, easing down until I'm sitting with the warm water covering me nearly to my shoulders.

The water is the perfect temperature, straddling that delicate edge of hot but not too hot, wonderfully.

"Join me?"

Bryce grabs the hem of his shirt, raising it above his head and discarding it on the floor before moving to his waistband. My eyes follow his movements intently, taking in the beautiful planes of his body as he strips off the rest of his clothes and then steps into the tub with me.

I settle myself between his legs, resting my back on his chest, my body melting into his as I relax.

Bryce traces shapes on my thigh with his finger, the cadence of his breaths steady as my body rises and falls with the movement of his chest.

"I love you," Bryce says, his voice low but earnest.

"I know," I murmur.

And I do.

I know without a shadow of a doubt that this man loves me wholly, even the pieces of me that I've tried so hard for him not to see. Every look, every touch, every action has been telling me the feelings of his heart long before he voiced the actual words right now.

I turn, shifting so that I'm straddling him and can look him in the eyes.

"I love you too."

His lips crash to mine, a hand coming up to cradle the back of my neck as we kiss feverishly. We break apart breathless, our foreheads pressed together as we both try to get oxygen to reach our lungs.

"I love you," Bryce repeats. "I need you to know that you never have to feel like you have to face anything alone ever again. I will be here for you always. You have my word."

We stay in the bath talking and enjoying each other's company until the water turns cool and my fingers and toes have long become wrinkly. I am about to suggest we get out when my stomach grumbles, reminding me that I never actually ate anything when I went on my quest for food.

Bryce chuckles a deep hearty laugh that I can feel vibrating through me. "Let's get you something to eat."

33
Epilogue - Sonny

I CUT THE ENGINE, the rumble of my Hellcat going quiet before I open the door and step out of the car. I haven't been here in longer than I'd like to admit. Before I could blame it on the distance or my busy schedule but now that I have moved back to Chicago, I have nothing to blame but myself. In total, I've only been here a handful of times but today I felt compelled to make the trip.

There are fresh flowers by the headstone, probably left by my mom or one of my sisters on one of their recent trips.

I place my hand on his headstone, feeling the coolness of the granite on my fingertips. "Hey dad."

It's cloudy and the air smells like rain is on its way, but I sit in the grass in front of my dad's headstone and just talk.

I talk about everything and nothing at all.

I tell him about the album. The success it's seen since it was released a few months ago. A couple of the songs charted well with one of them taking the number one spot and staying there for five straight weeks. So much success that I've been nominated for two awards, something that hasn't happened since my first album.

I tell him about how grateful I am that I came back home and how I'm thinking about selling my house in Los Angeles and buying something more permanent here.

Finally, I tell him about Laila.

I reach into my pocket and pull out the ring box I just picked up from the jeweler this morning. I rub my thumb across the black velvet of the box before I flip it open. Nestled in the cushions of the box is a three carat oval diamond engagement ring. Even in the dim light it sparkles.

"You would've loved her," I say, closing the box and putting it back in my pocket for safe keeping.

I stay a while longer, lost in thought before it's time for me to leave. I place another hand on my dad's headstone, promising him that I'll visit more often before I turn and walk back to my car.

***

Laila hasn't noticed me yet.

She's standing as still as a statue as her glam team moves around her, doing this and that to finish off her look for the award show tonight.

Her dress fits her to perfection, a black strapless gown with a plunging neckline that shows off just enough but isn't scandalous.

Her hair is pulled up into a sleek updo. The look is all brought together with her diamond accessories and gloves that go up to her elbows.

"You're beautiful," I say, making my presence known.

A smile instantly comes to her face as she looks over to where I'm standing.

"Thank you. You clean up well yourself," she says, her gaze taking a slow perusal down my body.

My stylists and I decided on a burgundy monochromatic suit look with shiny black shoes and I was happy with the outcome.

One of the women working on Laila rubs some sort of makeup stick along her shoulders and collarbone and then buffs it in with the largest makeup brush I've ever seen. Whatever it is, it leaves her body glowing as if she's out in the sunshine and not inside my spare room on a gloomy day.

Satisfied with her work, the woman takes a couple quick pictures and videos before she exits the room, leaving Laila and I alone.

"Don't look at me like that," Laila says.

"Like what?" I ask, feigning innocence.

"Like you want to destroy all of the hard work it took to get me to look like this and instead take me to bed."

I give her a devilish grin, happy that she knows me so well because that's exactly what I want to do.

"I mean...," I say, raising my eyebrows.

"Bryce!"

"Okay, okay we'll go. But once we get back, that ass is mine."

She rolls her eyes but I can tell she wants me just as much as I want her.

Traffic to the arena is terrible as usual but we eventually make it to the area designated for our drop off. I step out of the car and then extend my hand to Laila to help her out.

We make our way to the carpet but before we continue on, I stop and turn to look at her.

"Are you sure about this?" I ask, squeezing her hand.

It's loud, the buzz of people in conversation and the constant clicks of cameras but I want to be certain that this is what she wants.

I told her that she didn't have to walk the carpet with me, sure that she wouldn't want that much attention drawn to her, but she's been adamant that she will walk with me.

"I want to do this for you," she says. "This is a really important occasion and I want to be by your side for it."

My heart swells at her words and I'm reminded just how much I fucking love her.

One of the event assistants ushers us on to the carpet and guides us to the first mark to get our pictures taken. Once those have been taken, we continue our way down the carpet, stopping for more photos both together and some of just me alone. I do two quick interviews and Laila stands off to the side beaming at me with pride as I talk about my look for the night and the success of the album.

All of it is a blur of light and sound and I'm happy when we're finished and can go to our seats.

I glance around at the few people already seated at our table, some acquaintances I haven't had much interaction with, until my eyes land on Dez.

He pulls me into a one arm hug. "Thank God. I was gonna be bored out of my fucking mind with just those other people."

I chuckle at his sentiments before stepping back and introducing him to Laila. They greet each other and then we all take our seats.

Shortly after, the show begins.

My first nomination is one of the last awards presented, song of the year. The nominees list is stacked with talent including myself and Dez.

The presenter of the award comes on stage with the envelope.

"And the award goes to...," the presenter opens the envelope and leans into the mic.

"DEZ!"

I stand and clap, a big grin on my face, genuinely so happy for my friend. He daps me up and we hug before he makes his way through the audience and to the stage to accept his award and give his acceptance speech.

When he walks off stage, a commercial break starts and the crew starts to set up for the next performance. Everyone talks and mingles with the people around them while we wait.

Laila squeezes my hand to get my attention and I look over at her.

"I'm sorry you didn't win," she whispers.

I shake my head and smile. "Don't be. I already have everything I've ever dreamed of."